ROCK SOLID

A FOUNDATION COURSE IN YOUTH DRAMA FOR WORSHIP

ANNE COLLINS

Kevin Mayhew

First published in 1997 by
KEVIN MAYHEW LTD
Rattlesden
Bury St Edmunds
Suffolk IP30 0SZ

0 1 2 3 4 5 6 7 8 9

ISBN 1 84003 100 X
Catalogue No 1500160

Cover illustration by Kirstie Whiteford
Cover design by Jaquetta Sergeant
Edited by David Gatward
Typesetting by Louise Hill

Contents

This book is dedicated to the glory of God
and to all Mustard Seeds, past, present and future.

The Kingdom of Heaven is like this.
A man takes a mustard seed and sows it in his field.
It is the smallest of all seeds, but when it grows up,
it is the biggest of all plants. It becomes a tree,
so that birds come and make their nests in its branches.
Matthew 13:31-32

I assure you that if you have faith as big as a mustard seed,
you can say to this hill, 'Go from here to there!' and it will go.
You could do anything.
Matthew 17:20

Acknowledgements

This book is dedicated firstly to the glory of God, and secondly to all the Mustard Seeds scattered around England and indeed the world, especially South Africa. Thirdly it is a way of thanking all those who ever befriended us, watered us, fed us, pruned us, and cared for us over the years in Christian love, and all the friends from Theatre Church and St. Andrew's in Bolton. I remember especially our Christian friends in Devon and Cornwall who put up with 'Mustard Seed Mania' for several summers without complaint, fed us with wise words of fellowship (and pavlova), and with so much love. I thank, too, Darren, Helen, Fiona and Mark, who gave up so much of their time to help Mustard Seed in the early years, and to Dennis and Sally Burton who provided inspiration help. Finally I thank my husband Geoff for his patience and support without which the Seeds would never have been sown.

Introduction

The Reasons Why

In 1984, at Theatre Church, Bolton, a week of drama for 11-16 year olds was organised, because I felt prompted to use my experience in teaching and drama to explore issues such as justice and freedom, within a Christian context. It was meant to be a one-off experiment, just to see how things went. At the beginning of the week, a group of twenty-five nervous and not-so-nervous 11-16 year olds, from many different Christian denominations, gathered to play drama games, learn skills and improvise on the theme 'Bread not Bombs'. At the end of the week we put together a presentation for parents, a communication through dance, drama, poetry and music, about the burning issues with which that particular group were concerned, especially in relation to their Christian faith. The young people made up for lack of dramatic skills and technique with their directness, idealism, enthusiasm and refusal to compromise what they were told in the Bible with what they were told in the world, or indeed with their consciences! I returned home totally exhausted at the end of this hectic week, thinking, 'That's that then!'

But God had other ideas. The first phone call and an invitation to Burnley to repeat the performance pushed me into bringing the group together again. The second call asked me, out of the blue, for a name for the group, for their publicity purposes. Mustard Seed was the name which immediately sprang to mind! From that moment I was given responsibility for the dramatic development of a noisy, lively, questioning group of young people. Did I want it? I wasn't sure! The drama was OK, I could cope with that, but there was bound to be the frightening task of answering all their questions about Christianity. I didn't feel at all competent to deal with that, and knew that it would mean rather a lot of extra work to add to my already very busy life. Like Gideon, I kind of looked over my shoulder, thinking that there must be someone else to do the job. Like Jonah, I really would have

preferred to run very fast in the opposite direction, and stick to the safe, secular drama of plays and musicals, and normal 'Youth Theatre Workshop'. At least I would have my experience to draw on. God knew, however, that I had much to learn, and so, with trepidation, I faced my 'Nineveh'. My long-suffering husband sighed resignedly as I rushed headlong into the unknown, and clambered into the driving seat of the first of many broken-down old battle buses which he and other generous volunteers were to drive for miles during the next ten years, surrounded by the loud exuberance of a bunch of very normal teenagers!

This book is a compilation of some of the hundreds of sketches, tried and tested, which we devised together over those years. Despite all my fears and apprehension, I must state that it was a God-given privilege to work with these young people, a time when they taught me a great deal, and a part of my life I look back upon in amazement and joy. As a small community, we searched together for God's truth and found a closeness and love between us that I had never experienced before. Many of the original 'Seeds', though scattered all over the United Kingdom, and, indeed, the world, are still in contact, and I count many of them as my extended family, and amongst my greatest friends. Mustard Seed, and the way it developed, was indeed a gift from God – it wouldn't have grown as it did if we'd worked in our own strength instead of in his Spirit.

This is the first of two books of sketches, and is an attempt to share what we received, and to enable others to share our discoveries and learn from our mistakes. If new groups can gain from our experience, and communicate the Word of God clearly and forcefully, with humour and sincerity in our broken, disjointed world, then the 'seed' sown can continue to grow.

Mustard Seed went on to devise *Prisoners of Hope* and *The Man*, a multi-media rock musical which toured to Westminster Central Hall, Oxford, Loughborough, Bude and North

Devon, and Cornwall. Finally *The Man* was directed at the Market Theatre in Johannesburg, South Africa, in 1991, by a founder member of Mustard Seed, and performed by a mixed-race group to a mixed-race audience. This was the Lord working through people in a wonderful and most unexpected way. The nitty gritty work was done in Bolton and surrounding districts, leading services and raising money for charity.

The path God sets out for your group will be different, and according to the needs of the fellowship. Be open to his guidance and love, and he will help you to overcome obstacles, of which there will be many, I assure you. He will help you if you trust in him, and turn your weaknesses into strengths. I pray that these books will help you and the young people you work with, and that you will be truly blessed as we have been.

ANNE COLLINS

About the Author

Anne Collins lives in the North of England, and has been a teacher for over thirty years. She is married, with two children, both actors. She has retired from teaching as such, but works as an 'Artist in Schools', bringing her experience in drama skills to staff and pupils. From 1985 until 1993 she directed the Mustard Seed Drama Fellowship (an ecumenical group including young people from all denominations, plus those searching for faith), which appeared twice at MAYC, in the Westminster Central Hall, firstly with sketches similar to those in this book, and secondly with a production of *The Man*, a multimedia rock musical paralleling conditions of the world, with the person of Jesus Christ, and challenging all to 'stand up and be counted' alongside him against injustice, prejudice and cruelty.

She was also involved in Youth Theatre Workshops, writing full-scale productions with a message, such as *Snow Queen* (With God all things are possible), *Pinocchio* (New life is available for all), *Alice* (Be as a little child), creating original nativity scripts for church and school, and, as Head of Drama in a variety of schools, teaching. Her ministry with Mustard Seed included leading services, church weekends, and Drama in Worship courses. From this has arisen her latest project, 'Sowing Seeds', a kind of 'have workshop, will travel' idea. She also runs, along with Geoff, her husband, 'Drama Workshop', for young people aged eight upwards, which homes-in on drama skills, builds confidence and creates a good group experience for those involved. She and her husband attend St Andrew's Methodist Church in Bolton.

She hopes that this book, written from her experience, will be of use to those who feel called to communicate God's word through drama, and especially to those who are afraid to make the first move because of a lack of confidence.

Using This Book

This book consists of three sections:

1 **Workshops** which include drama skills and ideas which focus on the theme of the following sketch.

2 **Scripts** of original tried and tested Mustard Seed sketches on Old and New Testament themes.

3 **Director's Tips** which run parallel to each page of script and enlarge upon stage directions, and hopefully give ideas and ways of improving the performance itself.

The games, exercises, ideas and approaches within this book have been gleaned from a variety of sources over the years, many of them passed on to me orally and practically during my time as a teacher of Drama, as a director or simply by picking the brains of actor friends and other directors and practitioners, famous and unknown. Some of these games have evolved and changed, rather like 'Chinese Whispers' to suit occasions, themes and particular groups of people. No doubt these changes will continue as others take the ideas further. The skills, techniques and ideas, which are their essence, will, I hope, remain the same.

Over the years I have come up against the well-meaning, often enthusiastic, but, I feel, misguided attitude of, 'Let's do a sketch in the service tomorrow, it'll liven things up, and appeal to the young people'. One hour's preparation, and 'bingo' – it's performed, often with nervousness and embarrassed giggles from the young people. I would not go as far as to say that this never communicates God's word, because it often can. What I am saying is that it can be done better! Our God deserves the best that we can offer. So we must search our hearts and minds to seek his will, and work hard to learn the basic skills of good communication, so that we can tell his wonderful story with greater clarity. This isn't about 'performance', but about worship and the offering of ourselves wholly to God in his service.

The other important issue that this attitude to drama in worship masks, is that it is a creative process, which is not only a learning experience in terms of life skills, but also a very effective way of opening hearts and minds to God, and to others. When handed over to him, with a commitment to the search for his truth, and the determination to work hard, in his name – then impossible and wonderful things can and do happen. It acts as a crucible, into which the Lord can pour his Holy Spirit, and through his Son, lead us and guide us, teach us and restrain us. Without this approach Drama can be dangerous, and create mini 'stars', big 'egos' and uncaring attitudes. When this kind of work is pursued through prayer and fellowship, the quiet and shy can express their deep faith and gain confidence, the bold extrovert can learn to make way for others, the strong in faith can hold up the weak, the confident lead the nervous, and all can love each other and learn together in the name of Jesus.

Taking this way is not easy. It means meeting as a group on a regular basis at least for a reasonable length of time, a three-month or six-month project perhaps, to test the water, or a full-blown commitment to leap in and see where you are led! It means pooling skills, and exploring Christian belief with all its difficult questions and immense challenges to our lives. But the reward of communicating that faith in the best way you can, can bring others to God, raise awareness of issues, and galvanise people into action for God.

What Kind of Approach?

The sketches can be approached in many different ways, nothing is carved in marble! However, four ways of using this book come to mind, but I do believe that the 'Spiritual Warm-up', though basic, is essential to the whole process. What I have written is merely a suggestion and I feel sure that many of you will want to develop your own. This is great, as many of you will be given different insights, and that is right. However, I believe that there should always be a prayer time at the beginning and end of each workshop and each rehearsal.

The Four Approaches

1 For leaders who want to use drama, but really don't know whether they could cope! Start at the beginning and work right through the book with your group, and take time to do it, time to explore the ideas, and time to really grow in fellowship. I believe this is the best way of using this book, for all concerned. The reason is that all the sketches and workshops are arranged as far as possible in order of difficulty, and the games exercises and skills develop like-wise. You will find that games are repeated, but rather than have you skip back and forth from section to section, I have included reminders where necessary. This makes each workshop much more user-friendly.

2 For those who want to learn more, and improve communication skills. Take each story, in whatever order you wish, and lead into it through the workshop and fellowship. Begin the script, and use the Director's Tips to reinforce what you have learned.

3 For those with some experience. Choose a script with a theme which appeals, lean on the Director's Tips for direction, to help you to communicate the message more clearly, and to act as a safety net for your 'actors'. The group should have some basic drama skills.

4 For the highly experienced. Dip in at any point, and use the sketches, interpreting and staging them yourselves as you wish. This would be a reasonable approach for an older, experienced group.

Approaching the Script

1 Set the text in context. Explain what has happened just before, and just after. Explain any customs and cultural ideas which influence the story.

2 Always have a theological adviser when a second opinion is needed. Don't be afraid to ask for help.

3 Read through the script together (preferably after the preceding workshop is completed).

4 Cast the sketch. Remember that it is necessary sometimes to cast less-experienced and weaker members of the group in parts which will encourage them and help them to learn. Make sure that the more experienced are cast in a way that they can help the others and carry the important dialogue. Remember though, that everyone needs a challenge, and that sometimes you must cast and trust! This is the time to stress that everyone is as important as each other. Scotch any ideas that the one with the most lines is somehow superior to the others. Stress that the sketch is as strong as its weakest link.

5 Make sure that everyone understands stage directions (e.g. **DSR** means **D**own **S**tage **R**ight. **CS** means **C**entre **S**tage. See *Glossary* for in-depth explanation and *Stage Plan*.) Even if you are working in a small space, with a pulpit in the centre and pews in the acting area, this concept is vital.

6 Insist that everyone has a pencil to write in moves and alterations.

7 Roughly *block out* (see *Glossary*) the moves, taking into account the natural inclination of the actors, but always being aware of the status and tensions between characters, and the visual image. Feel your way through together. Alter positions where necessary and to suit your space. Refer back to workshop sessions and replay games and exercises where necessary.

8 Once moves are *blocked*, run through several times to consolidate and adjust. Watch out for:
masking
diction
character
levels
(See *Glossary* and *Workshops*).

9 Now begin to concentrate on how the action is performed, and develop the style as necessary.

10 Go with the flow if it works, but don't be afraid to put down the script and improvise when feeling is lost, or the focus is gone.

11 *Halfway House*. There is a point where no more improvement can be made until

scripts are down. Encourage this quickly. The sooner it happens the faster the progress, and the more everyone will enjoy it.

12 Work on beginnings and endings. Polish and add details.

13 Allow plenty of time to rehearse in the place where you are to present the sketch, and make adjustments accordingly. Use pews, chairs, blocks, aisles, etc., to make sure that everyone can see as well as hear.

Problems?

When facing problems, or arguments about interpretation which you sense is breaking down relationships or motivation *STOP*, and pray together. This will:

- Hand it over to God.
- Calm frayed nerves.
- Restore peace in equality before God.
- Heal relationships.
- Remind everyone why they are there – to worship and proclaim the Lord.
- Allow individual and personal problems to come into the open, before the Lord, to be shared, so that support can be given.
- Get all things into perspective. It is only a sketch after all!

Advice for the Leader

In a group such as this, there must be a democratic and caring approach, but the leader must have the final word. He can see the overall view, which members of the cast cannot. However, don't throw your weight around, approach all situations, as far as you can, with tolerance and love. (You won't manage it all the time – we are all human!) Always be honest if you don't know the answers.

And above all: *don't be afraid to ask for help!*

Size of Group

The workshops are designed for a group of around twelve, but should work for eight or sixteen. I wouldn't recommend working with less than six, and certainly, if you are new to this, with more than sixteen!

Workshops vary in length. You may want to spend more time on a section than it says. That's fine. Split the workshops into two or three sessions if you want to. But, if you do this, follow the guidelines below. You may find that some things take a little longer with one group than they do with another. I have tried to allow for this in my timings and hope that they are not too way out. You will speed up, with experience, and so will your group.

- Always dedicate your work as a group in prayer before you begin.
- Always lead into the work through relaxation, an energetic game, at least one concentration game and a revision of where you are at and what your aim is for the session.
- Always do this before *any* session, workshop, read through, or rehearsal. These things keep everything in its right perspective keeping the focus where it should be spiritually, physically and practically.
- Always finish by drawing the group together in prayer. The family that prays together, stays together! It's a cliché, but it is true!

Always allow some time at the end of the session for socialising, and try to follow up any pastoral needs at this time. As you progress, members of the group will begin to take on some responsibility for this too. It is wonderful to see the young people ministering to each other.

Surveying the Ground
A Foundation Workshop

THEME

Unity and Working together.

Duration

1 1/2 hours to 2 1/2 hours.

Building Materials

- Good News Bible
- Self-stick labels with everyone's first name written large and clear.
- Lively popular music
- Tape recorder/CD player.
- Cards with essence themes
- Cards with Quick Pic themes.

SPIRITUAL WARM-UP

10-15 minutes

Prayer and Dedication

Heavenly Father, we thank you for bringing us together to explore your Word through drama. We ask that you will bless us as we enter unknown territory, and that you will take our gifts, whatever they may be, that they may be used to your glory alone. Take away our fear and nervousness and help us to share all aspects of this fellowship in an atmosphere of support and love. In the name of Jesus, Amen.

Chorus

Father, I place into your hands the things that I can't do. (40, *Easy-to-Play Choruses*, Kevin Mayhew Ltd; and 121, *Hymns Old & New*, New Anglican Edition, Kevin Mayhew Ltd.)

Selecting the Plot

This workshop is intended to draw us closer together as a group, to break down barriers and to release us to learn new ideas and skills which will help us to be creative in our worship. It will help us to prepare and approach a script with more insight, and to learn new skills which will help us to communicate our own devised work in a more positive way. Hopefully it will also be a means in which we can celebrate each other's gifts, discover new ones of our own, and support and help each other as we work. Today's workshop is about getting to know each other and beginning to trust each other.

CHECKING THE MASTER PLAN

Read 1 Corinthians 12:12-26.

Discussion

- What do you think this passage means?
- How does this meaning affect us in our work together?
- Does the fact that we are all different, with different strengths and weaknesses, influence the way we respond to each other?

Foundation Stone 1

Everything is of value to God, even the things which have many mistakes, as long as they are offered openly and in the right spirit of worship. Some are natural leaders, and this is good. Some have confidence and others are shy. Some can be heard easily, others are quiet. If all work together and support each other in the spirit of love then with God all things are possible. Don't laugh at others, laugh with them. Co-operate in every way. Listen to each other.

GAMES

10 minutes

Hello Game – Breaking the Ice

Everyone into a space.

Give 30 seconds for the group to shake hands with everyone in the group and a further 30 seconds to say 'Hello, I'm (They say their name). How do you do?'

Now give one minute to invent a new way of saying hello, using nonsense words and sounds and a movement or movements to go with it. This *must* be done alone. E.g.: You could tap your head with your right hand while waving your left hand, bobbing up and down and saying, 'Ickly bob uck aaaargh. Wowow!' One minute to introduce yourself to everyone, using the new 'hello'.

Foundation Stone 2

It's important to relax and let yourself go. Don't be afraid to make a fool of yourself!

Name Game –
Concentration and Breaking the Ice

This is a CIRCLE game, and is played by establishing a rhythm.

First Stage – Slap knees twice, then click first the right hand and then the left parallel with shoulders. Keep a slow steady rhythm going. The group will want to speed up, but must remain slow in order to cope with the next stage.

Second Stage – On the right click call out your own name, before clicking the left hand say, 'to', and then as the left hand is clicked call out the name of another person in the circle. For example, 'Fred (as RH clicks) to Mary (as LH clicks).'

Foundation Stone 3

Emphasise a steady rhythm. Be sure to include everyone. Clear voice projection.

PREPARING THE GROUND

5-10 minutes

Breathing and Relaxation

All to lie flat on backs in a space away from each other. It is important that they are relaxed with hands by sides, fingers unclenched, legs uncrossed and feet flopping outwards. Close eyes.

Ask them to think through the events of the day, and imagine that they have a suitcase into which they can fold them and put them away. Then they must imagine that the lid on the suitcase is shut and their minds uncluttered, and ready to begin the workshop.

Breathe in as deeply as possible, through the nose (asthma sufferers may find this hard, so adapt). Then let the breath go out through the mouth. Do this five times.

Get them to put their hands on their diaphragm and feel the lungs expanding the rib cage. Get them to imagine that a magnet is making them feel incredibly heavy as it pulls them through the floor. They cannot move as all their body is heavy.

Ask them to stretch their hands taut and then relax them. Work through the body isolating as far as possible each set of muscles, stretching and relaxing them. Hands, hands and arms, feet, feet and legs, stomach muscles, shoulders, chest, neck, and finally all face muscles (open eyes and mouth wide, stretch tongue, etc).

Now stretch the whole body and relax, twice. Slowly sit up.

This is a good place for the leader to introduce, or remind the group of the concept of NEUTRAL which is mentioned many times throughout the workshops and 'tips' later on. (See *Foundation Stone 4*.)

Finally ask them to move around the room in a NEUTRAL way, without reacting to people they pass in any way, as if in a world of their own! Very hard – takes much practice.

Foundation Stone 4

It is worth spending time on the initial part of this exercise. Emphasise the body and voice as an instrument of communication. Explain how the voice is produced through vocal chords, and pressure of breath. Explain how important it is to be able to control the voice, facial expressions and body shape when communicating through drama. Emphasise self-control and self-discipline. Parallel with training in sports or music, etc. It takes practice!

Neutral is just the state of 'being yourself at rest', not fidgeting, or drawing attention to yourself, or becoming another character. It is a state of non-acting, of waiting, relaxed, but in readiness, so that you can be galvanised into action when the need arises. It is a stillness, a temporary 'being laid aside'. Stillness is really important, and is very different from being in a 'freeze', which is often tense and definitely 'focused'. They need to stand with feet slightly apart, hands by sides, and remember the feeling after stretching all the muscles during the breathing exercises. They should try to recapture this in an upright position.

VOICE WARM-UP

3-5 minutes

A-E-I-O-U

Lie in a space on the floor.

Bring knees up so that feet are flat on the floor.

Take a deep breath (as in breathing and relaxation) and softly sing any note to the sound of ay, taking more breaths where necessary, controlling the output of breath as long as possible and changing to ee, then iy, oh and oo.

Finally, using the change of sounds in own time, *chew* on the sounds and spit them out. Notice what happens to the sound as the shape of the mouth changes, and as the amount of breath increases and decreases.

Foundation Stone 5

Use the mouth, don't sing through the teeth, notice the different shapes the mouth makes for each sound. Think of the mouth cavity as a megaphone. Stress using facial muscles and how it affects use of voice.

SHAKE OUT

5 minutes

Using a popular CD or cassette with a good medium to fast rhythm, shake out hands, arms, legs, hips, face. Finish by moving in any way to the rhythm.

All stand in a space. Shake right hand, then left hand, feet, hips, shoulders, heads and whole body in time to the music. Stretch high, touch toes (Mr Motivator's got nothing on this!) at least ten times.

Now roll head round slowly to the left in a full circle, then to the right. Repeat five times each. Slowly, vertebra by vertebra, beginning with the base of the neck and working down, bend from the waist. Then swing arms to the right and to the left five times each, finally slowly uncurl to standing position, vertebra by vertebra, beginning at the base of the spine.

Finally, move into a circle, and each member of the group devises a simple (but energetic, please!) movement which is copied by the others.

Foundation Stone 6

Emphasise whole-hearted, not half-hearted movement, with energy. Stress imaginative movement at different levels. Introduce the idea of different levels, high, medium, low, and the use of space.

WORK IN PAIRS

10 minutes

HEAD-TO-HEAD

In pairs, sit facing each other in a space, close enough to be heard when speaking quietly, and far enough away from others to hold a private conversation. In one minute (timed carefully) tell as much as possible on each theme.

Decide who is A and who is B and take it in turns to have one minute's speaking time. Change partners for each theme.

Themes:
  My family
  My most frightening/embarrassing experience, and why
  If I had a million pounds I would . . .
  Things I dislike.

13

Foundation Stone 7

Inevitably the majority will not finish their stories and the leader should suggest that they resume the conversations at another time. Stress the importance of being oneself, and the confidentiality of the conversations. Stress the need to think fast, speak quickly, but clearly in order to get the information over. Don't stray from the subject. If someone dries up, the other can ask a question. Trust and support each other.

WORK IN GROUPS

20 minutes

QUICK PICS

Divide the group into threes or fours.

Give them 15 seconds to create a visual image of the following themes. (Leader counts down the seconds). On the count of fifteen the command FREEZE is given, and the leader gives points to the best three. Encourage the use of different levels and shapes. A drum comes in handy here as a signal and it also saves your voice!

Foundation Stone 8

LEVELS – The use of levels is quite a simple concept. It means using different physical positions at different heights. E.g. lying flat on the floor is the lowest level, stretching up, standing on tiptoe is the highest level, standing normally is the middle level, and the other levels are points in between.

These can be achieved purely by the actors' physical position in relation to each other, or can be enhanced with the use of chairs, blocks, pews, pulpit, or whatever is at hand. As we look at a picture, our eye is drawn around it by the placing of various objects, and/or their colour.

We focus on a contrast, or something towards which the objects or people are gesturing or pointing. In order to do this, and to lead the eye of the beholder towards that which we want them to view (that was a mouthful!), we place people and things at different levels.

Themes
All groups:
  Giraffe
  Ice-cream cone
  Tree in a strange forest.

Individual groups:
(Given a card with their quick pic on it)
  Snake
  Jaws
  Fire
  Bridge
  Pop group
  Road accident.

SHARING

Let each group show their Quick Pic, and get the rest to guess the theme, then discuss briefly the merits of each group.

Foundation Stone 9

Importance of physical contact without embarrassment. Working efficiently, no time to argue. Using imagination in the use of LEVELS. Being open to the ideas of others. 'Freeze' means no movement at all. Introduction of the term VISUAL IMAGE, with reference to adverts and symbols.

WHOLE GROUP WORK

50 minutes

WALKING INTO PICTURES

This is an extension of Quick Pics involving the whole group, which covers a variety of basic skills, with an end result (using other more appropriate themes) which can be used easily to illustrate a text or an abstract theme.

The group is asked to sit at one end of the working space, all facing towards the stage area. They must imagine a picture frame stretching from floor to ceiling and from wall to wall. Tell them that they are going to create their own picture in FREEZE FRAME based upon the given theme. At a given signal they move into the frame, and take up the position of an appropriate character or object.

14

Themes:
  At the zoo
  Emergency ward at the hospital.

Foundation Stone 10

After the first attempt when all will probably rush in without thinking, or have to be helped with ideas, discuss ways in which improvements could be made.

Consider the following:- LEVELS, accurately mimed positions, co-operation between different members of the group. Introduce the word MASKING (standing in front of someone so that they cannot be seen).

Talk about the picture as a TABLEAU. Adjust and alter, at the suggestion of the group. Encourage them to be animals, railings, cages, people involved in activities together and alone. Get them to think about their facial expressions, and what they are feeling.

Try again with the second theme asking them to bear in mind all the things discussed. Praise and be positive, pick out the good things, and encourage the group to do the same. If necessary, the leader will have to tell each person when to go into the picture, bearing in mind that some people need longer to think than others!

ESSENCE MACHINES

Divide them into groups of no more than five and no less than three. Ask how they can tell the difference between different ice creams or drinks. Introduce the word ESSENCE and draw the parallel between types of ice-cream and different themes or types of scene in a play.

Show an example by picking four demonstrators, and placing them in a line. Each helper must think of a sentence or phrase on a given theme, e.g. At the Seaside.

Get them to speak their sentence or phrase. Ask them then to think of an action to go with it. Encourage the others to make suggestions. Repeat the words and actions over and over several times and make the point that machines are repetitive.

Ask everyone to suggest ways of making it look more interesting. Here are some suggestions:

- People at different heights and positions in the acting area. (A bit like mini Walking into Pictures!)
- More expressive faces and voices
- Being a character or showing the mood more clearly

Then, when you are sure that they understand the procedure, give each group a card with a theme on it. They must use the same procedure to get to the essence of the idea, and create a machine as demonstrated. Time restricted to 10 minutes maximum.

Themes:
  Haunted house
  Shopping
  Christmas
  Winter
  Friendship
  Old people
  Bonfire Night.

Foundation Stone 11

Use one group to demonstrate an 'essence machine' with the theme 'At the Seaside'. Firstly, stand them in a line and ask them to think of a word or phrase, or activity to describe 'At the Seaside', such as, 'Let's go for a swim', 'Mummy, can I have an ice cream?' 'Aw! I've got sand in my drink!' 'Brrrr! The sea's cold.' These sentences do not have to be related. Run it through in order, repeating it over and over like a machine. Secondly, ask them to think of an action to go with their phrase. Run it through in order. Ask the rest how the demonstrators could make it more interesting to watch. Get them to refer back to levels, masking, accurate mime, etc. Encourage the rest to direct the changes, until the sequence is easily recognisable.

SHARING

Present Essences and try to guess themes.

Foundation Stone 12

Being a good audience. Learning from others. Observing.

BUILDING INSPECTION

- Discuss positives.
- Discuss possible improvements.

Foundation Stone 13

Always encourage the group to be positive and constructive in their criticisms, so go for the good things first. Then look at the negative things under the umbrella of possible improvements. This is a much less threatening way of dealing with presentations. 'It's not what you say, it's the way that you say it!'

You will probably find that the group tends to be negative in their criticism at first. Don't allow it. Make them use the terminology you require and encourage truthful but generous comment at all times.

If someone is deliberately fooling about, which often happens, tell them in no uncertain terms that they are being destructive, but try to assess why they are behaving this way before you wade in too heavily, for giggles and laughter often are signs of embarrassment and nerves.

Consider the following:
- *Can it be heard?*
- *Is the visual communication accurate?*
- *Is the mime believable?*
- *Are the group really concentrating?*
- *Are they making the best use of levels?*
- *Is there evidence of good group co-operation?*

Stress that they should be critical without being unkind; positive and constructive not negative and destructive. All offerings are valuable because everyone has something to offer, and something to learn.

CLOSING PRAYER

3-5 minutes

Lord, we thank you for the time we have had together, and for the things we have learned. For new friends and new ideas we give you thanks. Amen.

The Lord's Prayer.

The Peace.

Ab and Isaac – Workshop
Genesis 22:1-19

THEME

Obedience and trust.

DURATION

2 hours 50 minutes to 3 hours. Could be split easily into two workshops of 1½ to 2 hours each.

BUILDING MATERIALS

Bible
Tape recorder/cassette player
Story Board cards

SPIRITUAL WARM-UP

10-15 minutes

PRAYER AND DEDICATION

Lord, we come together to worship you using our individual gifts and abilities. Help us to understand your word more clearly, as we work, and to see where it affects our own lives today. We ask you to concentrate our minds and hearts, and to help us to work together in harmony. We dedicate this time to your glory. In the name of Jesus Christ Our Lord, Amen.

CHORUS

Be Still. (11, *Easy-to-Play Choruses*, Kevin Mayhew Ltd; and 53, *Hymns Old & New*, New Anglican Edition, Kevin Mayhew Ltd.)

PREPARING THE GROUND

10 minutes

BREATHING AND RELAXATION

Play a quiet piece of music during this exercise.

All to lie flat on backs in a space away from each other. It is important that they are relaxed with hands by sides, fingers unclenched, legs uncrossed and feet flopping outwards with eyes closed.

Ask them to think through the events of the day, and imagine that they have a suitcase into which they can fold them and put them away.

Foundation Stone 1

Abraham was strong in faith, but we often find it hard to do God's will. But, because of Christ's death on the cross, we are forgiven, if we are truly sorry, and the slate is wiped clean.

As they think about recent events, ask them to think of all the occasions when they have been disobedient, to parents, at school or work, to God, and also think of times when they have lacked trust in someone, or in God. Ask God for forgiveness, and pack these things away in the imaginary suitcase.

Then they must imagine that the lid on the suitcase is shut, they are forgiven, and their minds uncluttered, and ready to begin the workshop.

Breathe in as deeply as possible, through the nose. (Asthma sufferers may find this hard, so adapt.) Then let the breath go out through the mouth. Do this five times. Get them to put their hands on their diaphragm and feel the lungs expanding the rib cage. Get them to imagine that a magnet is making them feel incredibly heavy as it pulls them through the floor. They cannot move as all their body is heavy.

Ask them to stretch taut only their hands and then relax them, work through the body isolating as far as possible each set of muscles, stretching and relaxing them. Hands, hands and arms, feet, feet and legs, stomach muscles, shoulders, chest, neck, and finally all face muscles (open eyes and mouth wide, stretch tongue, etc).

Finally stretch the whole body and relax, twice. Slowly sit up.

WORK IN PAIRS

20-30 minutes

HEAD-TO-HEAD

In pairs, sit facing each other in a space, close enough to be heard when speaking quietly, and far enough away from others to hold a private conversation.

In one minute (timed carefully) tell as much as possible on the following themes:

- What makes you want to disobey and rebel?
- Describe an incident when disobedience got you into trouble!
- Decide who is A and who is B and take it in turns to have one minute's speaking time, changing partners for each theme.

Foundation Stone 2

We are all dependent upon one another at some time. People trust us, we trust others. Sometimes a life may depend on this, you never know. We must learn to be responsible for each other, to care and support, to be there when needed. God is always there for us. Abraham realised that God's will was more important than anything else, and learned to be obedient and have faith. After all, Sarah had had a child when she was very old, and Abraham must have seen this as a special miracle from God, and a sign that God was with him in all situations. (Genesis 17:15-27, 18:11-14 and 21:1-7)

TRUST

10-15 minutes

Everyone into groups of three, ideally of similar height and weight. Decide who is to be A, B, and C.

A and B stand in a line behind each other and C directly faces them. B stands with feet together hands across chest and eyes closed. The aim is for A and C to rock B gently to and fro, gradually increasing the distance between them. B must keep body rigid, and rock on balls of feet to heels as he/she is pushed.

Foundation Stone 3

It must be made an enjoyable experience for the person in the centre. It must be stressed that it is not a competition to see who can fall the furthest, but an exercise in trust and care for each other. Some will fall almost to the ground, others will only cope for a short time. This is not a personal failure. If anyone loses concentration at any time, all must stop and either A or B goes into the centre to start again. Continue until all have had a turn.

VOICE WARM-UP

20-30 minutes

A-E-I-O-U

Lie in a space on the floor. Bring knees up so that feet are flat on the floor. Take a deep breath (as in breathing and relaxation) and softly sing any note to the sound of ay, taking more breaths where necessary, and controlling the output of breath as long as possible. Change to ee, then iy, oh and oo.

Finally, using the change of sounds in own time, CHEW on the sounds and spit them out, notice what happens to the sound as the shape of the mouth changes, and as the amount of breath increases and decreases.

Experiment with group sensitivity here. Ask them all to begin very quietly, then listening to each other, gradually reach a crescendo, and then, hardest of all, slowly go down to pianissimo again.

Remember to remind them that they can take a breath at any time.

Foundation Stone 4

Emphasise the need for clear speech and good diction. Explain that the mouth is like a cavern which echoes with any sound, and that it is important to use it as a sounding board. Explain that few of us use our mouths and jaws in the right way to gain maximum use of it, and that these exercises help us to speak more clearly and to project our voices better.

CHEWY TOFFEE TONGUE-TWISTER

In a circle, leader joining in, imagine that you have a very large piece of toffee in your mouth. Chew it, stretching jaws, etc. This will cause great amusement at first, but encourage self-control! Stick tongue out as far as possible (much dribbling here – be prepared) and touch chin, nose, then right cheek, followed by left cheek. Repeat several times.

Foundation Stone 5

After the dribbles have been wiped away, ask them to tell you how different the inside of their mouth feels. Answer: aching, larger, stretched. If they don't feel this way, then they need to stretch even more.

Now repeat the following words with tongue stuck out as far as possible. Try to keep the words as clear as possible (even more dribbling!) Repeat again normally, but using your mouth in an exaggerated way.

Father Abraham has many sons
Many sons has Father Abraham
I am one of them and so are you
So let's all praise the Lord.
Teach the tune of Father Abraham. (See page 64.)

Foundation Stone 6

Emphasise clear diction.

FUN GAME

In a circle repeat this song with the following additions and actions:
'Father Abraham has many sons
Many sons has Father Abraham
I am one of them and so are you
So let's all praise the Lord. *Right arm!*'
(*Swing right arm backwards and forwards with great energy. Keep it going as you repeat the verse again*)
End each verse with a different part of the anatomy, adding the action while still keeping the other parts of the body moving. This is a

good physical shake-out too. Even though everyone will end up totally confused at first, with practise it does get better. *Trust me!*
'Father Abraham has many sons
Many sons has Father Abraham
I am one of them and so are you
So let's all praise the Lord. *Right arm! Left arm!*'
(*swing left* and *right arms as you continue to sing the next verse.*)
At the end of every verse following, add a new movement as follows:
Right leg (*stamp right foot and continue to swing arms*)
Left leg (*Stamp left foot, then right foot plus arms*)
Turn around (*Keeping all other movements going*)
Nod your head (*Still keeping all movements going*)
Repeat the song once more with all the actions and of course *brilliant* diction!

Foundation Stone 7

Co-ordination is a vital skill which needs a great deal of practice. Diction and clear speech should be like second nature. When presenting anything, the actor must be aware of many things at the same time, and should be able to control body and voice at the same time.

WHOLE GROUP WORK

20-30 minutes

Foundation Stone 8

It is important when approaching any acting task to be able to use your imagination, and to draw on your own experiences and emotions in order to create characters which are believable. There is much thought involved in successful communication through drama. Exchange of ideas and feelings without embarrassment is vital too. All should be open to one another, and be prepared to go below the surface in terms of feelings and emotions. Let your hair down! Don't be afraid. Trust each other, and respect each other. None of the personal revelations occurring here should go beyond these walls. It is a privilege to share the innermost feelings of others, and one which we should not abuse.

IMPROVISATION

All sit in a space alone with eyes closed, and think of the most important person in your life. Visualise them. Think about the time you spend together. What do you like about them? Why are they special to you?

Stand up and face in different directions. Walk, changing directions every time the signal is given, still keeping this person in your mind. At the stop signal, turn to the nearest person and tell them about this person and why they are so important to you.

Now, sit in a space again, with eyes closed. Imagine this person. They are about to be taken away from you. How do you feel? What do you want to do to the person who is doing this to you?

Stand up and face in different directions. Walk, changing directions every time the signal is given, still keeping this person in your mind. At the stop signal, turn to the nearest person and tell them how you feel. Comfort each other.

(Sometimes this can be quite emotional, so the leader must be listening in, and joining in where necessary.)

MIME WALK

Imagine you are on a journey, but you are walking on the spot. Mime walk – put ball of foot down, followed by heel as you come up on the ball of the other foot, and so on.

Imagine you can see different people as you walk along, let your expression show your feelings. Imagine you are walking towards something you really want, and are excited about.

Then imagine that you don't want to go on this journey. How does this affect your posture and general movement?

Walk up a hill, then down a hill, think what happens to your body.

Sit in a space again, and imagine that you have to do something which will mean never seeing a special person ever again. How do you feel

about doing this? You have a choice to make. Will you take the necessary step or won't you?

DISCUSSION

Sit in a circle and share some of your feelings with each other. If this is difficult, write them down, put the papers in a hat, draw them out at random, read them and discuss.

Think about Abraham's feelings when he was asked to sacrifice Isaac, the son he never thought he would have. What thoughts must have gone through his head?

In facing these thoughts and feelings, did he show great courage and faith when he decided to take the hard way of obedience? Or do you think it was just an instant decision? If so did this show as much, or greater courage and faith?

WORK IN GROUPS

40-50 minutes

QUICK PICS

Divide the group into threes or fours. They are given 15 seconds to create a visual image of the following themes. (Leader counts down the seconds.) On the count of fifteen the command FREEZE is given, and the leader gives points to the best three. Encourage them to use LEVELS and imaginative body shapes; discourage straight lines.

Themes:
  Fire
  Trust
  Mistrust
  Bush
  Loving family
  Fear
  Celebration

Foundation Stone 9

Remember Levels? The use of levels is quite a simple concept. It means using different physical positions at different heights. E.g. lying flat on the floor is the lowest level, stretching up, standing on tiptoe is the highest level, standing normally is the middle level, and the other levels are points in between. These can be achieved purely by the actors' physical position in relation to each other, or can be enhanced with the use of chairs, blocks, pews, pulpit, or whatever is at hand. As we look at a picture, our eye is drawn around it by the placing of various objects, and/or their colour. We focus on a contrast, or something towards which the objects or people are gesturing or pointing. In order to do this, and to lead the eye of the beholder towards that which we want them to view (that was still a mouthful!), we place people and things at different levels.

STORY BOARDING

Read the story of Abraham and Isaac. Discuss in small groups the main points of the story. Give each group two cards with an aspect of the story, and the Bible reference. Ask each group to prepare a tableau or quick pic which communicates that aspect.

MAIN POINTS

1 God speaks to Abraham about the sacrifice of Isaac (Genesis 22:1-3).
2 The journey (Genesis 22:4-5).
3 Father and Son (Genesis 22:6-8).
4 Isaac is bound to the altar (Genesis 22:9-10).
5 The angel speaks (Genesis 22:11-12).
6 The ram in the bush (Genesis 22:13-14).
7 Blessings and Celebration (Genesis 22:15-18).

(This in itself is a simple, yet effective way of communicating this story.)

Foundation Stone 10

Remember to remind them that visual images can say as much, if not more, than words. Don't get bogged down in detail. If they are stuck, go back to the story board and develop those ideas. Cut out any unnecessary dialogue.

SHARING

Watch each tableau in order, reading the verses as they freeze in position.

BUILDING INSPECTION

• Discuss positives.
• Discuss ways of improvement.

Foundation Stone 11

Always encourage the group to be positive and constructive in their criticisms, so go for the good things first. Then look at the negative things under the umbrella of possible improvements. This is a much less threatening way of dealing with presentations. 'It's not what you say, it's the way that you say it!'

You will probably find that the group tends to be negative in their criticism at first. Don't allow it. Make them use the terminology you require.

Encourage truthful comment at all times.

If someone is deliberately fooling about, which often happens, tell them in no uncertain terms that they are being destructive, but try to assess why they are behaving this way before you wade in too heavily, for giggles and laughter often are signs of embarrassment and nerves.

Consider the following:
• *Can it be heard?*
• *Is the visual communication accurate?*
• *Is the mime believable?*
• *Are the group really concentrating?*
• *Are they making the best use of levels?*
• *Is there evidence of good group co-operation?*
• *Stress – Be critical without being unkind. Positive and constructive not negative and destructive. All offerings are valuable. Everyone has something to offer, and something to learn.*

CLOSING PRAYER

5 minutes

Lord, we thank you that you are always there, guiding us and keeping us safe, even when we feel threatened. We thank you too that all of us are valued and loved by you. Help us to value and love each other with all our strengths and weaknesses. Help us to appreciate each other's efforts. We ask that you will give us greater faith and trust in you, as we go our separate ways. In the name of Jesus Christ our Lord, Amen

The Grace

Ab and Isaac – A Sketch
Genesis 22:1-19

Characters: Ab, Isaac, Chorus A, B, C, D, E.

	(*The scene opens with a freeze frame Centre Stage*) **(1)**
Chorus D	(*Moves slightly away from tableau, addresses audience*) Abraham and Isaac, Father and son **(2)**
All	(*Remain frozen, but turn heads briefly to audience, then resume original position*) Loved each other dearly **(3)**
Chorus D	So said everyone!
Chorus A	(*Moving DSR*) They *really* love each other those *two*. **(4)**
Chorus B	They do, don't they! **(4)**
Chorus A and B	(*Glancing at each other*) They certainly do! **(5)**
Ab and Isaac	We certainly do! **(6)**
	(*Isaac and Chorus D, C and E move into neutral. Ab kneels in prayer*). **(7)**
Chorus C	(*Moving DSL*) An angel said to Ab **(8)**
Chorus A	(*Commandingly, as angel*) Take Isaac today.
Ab	(*reacts to the message from God*) **(9)**
Chorus A	Take him to a mountain, far away. God asks you to do this. So take this advice, and make your son Isaac a sacrifice.
Ab	No! (*Horrified*) **(10)**
Chorus A	Yes. (*Persuasively and gently*)
Ab	No. (*Worriedly shaking his head*)
Chorus A	Yes! (*Firmly*)

Director's Tips

(1) It is vital that everyone is totally 'frozen', so that the audience can focus upon the meaning of the interaction within the group, which sets the scene for the story. Ab's love for Isaac and Isaac's respect for his father must come across here, setting the scene for the story. The picture must be visually interesting, having different levels, the main focus must be on father and son.

(2) The narrators must take the audience into their confidence right from the start, so that they feel involved. Don't talk to a fixed point, take in the whole of the audience.

(3) Turn heads briefly at *exactly* the same time, look directly at the audience, then straight back to tableau after 'dearly', except Chorus D, who speaks directly to the audience, and Chorus A who moves away.

(4) Speak this really patronisingly, like a doting parent to a spoiled child. Emphasise the italicised words.

(5) This should be even more patronising, as if Ab and Isaac are little children. The actors should assume that the audience is with them, but in fact their sympathies will probably be with the two main characters.

(6) Ab and Isaac must, from the outset, play their roles with honesty, in contrast with the Chorus, who change role and attitude frequently. Ab and Isaac are constant in both senses of the word. They are irritated here by the attitude of the Chorus, and this must show in their tone of voice. Of course, Chorus A and B react in exaggerated amazement that they have caused offence.

(7) Moving into neutral. (See *Surveying the Ground – Foundation Workshop, Foundation Stone 4.*) Move into a position with backs to the audience where you do not MASK the action (See *Foundation Workshop, Foundation Stone 10.*) Put hands by sides, feet slightly apart. Relax and be still, as any movement or twitching, scratching heads or swaying, will distract from the focus of the action. This is a good method of changing from one character to another, and can be used to great advantage when there are large numbers in the cast and limited numbers within the group!

(8) Chorus A changes character as an angel. If desired Chorus A can go into neutral after the line 'They certainly do', and turn as the angel, thus focus will be drawn to the angel at the right time. The angel must be serious, and commanding, totally different from the Narrator role.

(9) Ab falls to his knees in prayer, looking up to heaven, not at the angel. He freezes, and we should see in his posture all the wonder of listening to God, combined with the inner struggle, and conflicting thoughts which must have gone through his head. These should be seen fleetingly in his expression.

(10) This must be genuine horror and disbelief, not 'over the top' exaggeration. The angel must begin fairly gently and firmly ending commandingly on the final 'Yes'. Ab should reflect on his face the struggle and then the obedience which his faith in God dictates to him.

Ab	No. *(Weakening)*
Chorus A	Yes! *(Strongly)*
Ab	*(Positively)* All right then. *(Ab stands. Chorus A moves USR into neutral)* **(11)**
	(Isaac turns and moves to Ab miming the carrying of wood on his shoulders. Ab mimes the carrying of food. Both walk in mime CS. Chorus D turns and watches the action.) **(12)**
Chorus C	Ab carried food, Isaac carried wood.
Chorus D	Ab did as God had asked.
Chorus C	*(Patronisingly)* Wasn't he good?
Ab	*(Firmly puts Chorus C in his place)* I always obey God *(walks and addresses audience)*.
Chorus D	As they walked along together, young Isaac cried.
Isaac	We haven't got a sacrifice! *(They stop and look at each other.)*
Ab	*(Confidently)* God will provide. *(Ab mimes constructing altar.)* **(13)**
Isaac	Dad built an altar, piled up the wood.
Ab	Isaac lit the fire, *(stands back and watches Isaac)* as I told him that he should.
Chorus D	Ab's eyes filled with tears *(Ab turns away, begins to sharpen his knife in mime.)* **(14)**
All Chorus	Boo hoo! **(15)**
Chorus D	As he sharpened his knife
Chorus A, B, D	*(Knife sharpening sounds accompanied by action)* **(16)**
Chorus C	And sadly prepared to offer his son's life.

(11)   As Ab says 'All right then', it must be in a positive, not a reluctant way. Abraham trusts God. After all, God gave him Isaac in very miraculous circumstances, and Abraham would obey God. However, he is human, and would not joyfully approach this task! His obedience and faith appears all the stronger because it is in spite of the situation in which he finds himself!

(12)   Mime and mime walk. (See *Ab and Isaac Workshop, Mime walk.*) The mime must be believable. They must pick up the items they carry from the floor. Make sure that the weight and size do not vary as they move. Drama is about accurate communication, and has to be worked on and refined. There is nothing worse than wafty ineffectual mime.

(13)   Altar: this could take the form of a small block placed in position from the beginning, or two chairs will be adequate, and can also be carried as wood and coal, by Ab and Isaac. Snag: the use of these can slow the action. Advantage: they can be used for different levels during the piece and do serve the purpose of raising the 'altar' reasonably high from the audience's point of view. You can use the chorus to form the altar, but they have to remain still for so long, it could cause problems. Experiment and choose what works best for your group.

(14)   Ab turns away, bows his head and then takes out his knife (*mime*) with determination. This must not be 'hammed' or overdone, but must be real and full of feeling. However, it must be large in movement and expression, as it has to communicate further than the front row!

(15)   All Chorus, except D turn to look at Ab and then at the audience, speaking 'Boo Hoo' as if they are children mocking. This may raise a laugh, but it should be against the Chorus and pro Ab. Exaggerated physical interpretation should go alongside.

(16)   Action in unison here, which must be 'larger than life' and finish in a freeze as Chorus C says 'life'.

(Ab finishes sharpening knife)

Chorus B Ab said to Isaac,

Ab Climb on the fire, while I build the wood a little bit higher.

Isaac *(Thinking it's a joke)* No. *(Laughing)* **(17)**

Ab *(Sadly)* Yes.

Isaac No! *(Objecting as he realises Ab means it)* **(18)**

Ab Yes! *(Firmly)*

Isaac No! *(Afraid)*

Ab Yes. *(Commandingly)* **(19)**

Isaac *(Looks at Ab trustingly)* Oh! All right then. **(20)**

(Isaac lies across altar. Ab moves behind it.)

Chorus B Ab took his knife

Chorus A And lifted it high. **(21)**

Chorus C He cried out to God, 'Does Isaac have to die?' **(22)**

Chorus B Just at that moment *(Chorus A, C and B become a 'bush' and Chorus D hides behind them)* **(23)** Out of a bush

Chorus A Came a big fat ram. All of a rush!

Chorus D *(Dashes from 'bush', is caught on 'thorns'. All in frozen amazed tableau.)* **(24)**

Chorus C God said to Ab.

Chorus A *(As angel)* Because of your trust, I won't reduce young Isaac to dust. **(25)**

Ab *(Gesturing with relief to ram)* Shall I use this then?

Chorus D No! *(Terrified)* **(26)**

(17) As in note 11, action here must be believable. The audience must see the range of emotions felt by Ab and Isaac. Pace is important in this sequence, it should not be laboured, cues picked up promptly. (See *In the Bag Workshop, Catch that Cue.*)

(18) The different meanings of each 'No' of Isaac's must be clear to the audience. Encourage large movement and larger-than-life expression, but do not allow it to become caricatured! The truth of feeling *must* show through.

(19) This must come over very much in father to son mode, reflecting the earlier relationship of God to Abraham. A strong gesture towards the altar might emphasise this if tone of voice doesn't appear to be enough.

(20) Isaac's trust of his father must show through. So 'All right then' must not be sulky, or angry, but with a resigned sigh and puzzled trust. Isaac too is obedient.

(21) This is the high point of the story, and the movement should be slow and dramatic. Ab should look very strong physically and spiritually at this point. A slight pause just before the knife is raised will add to the tension. All chorus *must* be still and focused on the action.

(22) Ab freezes, knife poised, closes his eyes, and then, as if hearing God's voice again and taking strength, he lifts the knife higher ready for the final blow.

(23) Chorus B must jump in on cue very fast, or Isaac will be killed, and then catastrophe! Immediately as he speaks, the other chorus move swiftly into the 'bush'. (See *Foundation Workshop, Quick Pics.*) Chorus D hides behind them. All focus will be drawn to the bush, especially if the shape is grotesque and spiky. It is vital that the dialogue which follows has great pace and energy of delivery, and that cues are picked up fast, otherwise the comic element will be lost, and it is often through comedy that we can understand the seriousness of an action or idea.

(24) As the 'ram' is 'caught' on a hand *(shaped like a thorn)*, Chorus A, B and C show facial expressions of utter amazement, and the ram looks very annoyed. Ab turns and lets the knife drop to his side, while Isaac cranes his neck to see what is happening.

(25) Chorus A as the Angel must move away from the bush and adopt 'angel' stature. All look at him/her so that attention is focused on what he/she says. Angel speaks on the move, finally turning to look at Ab and the altar. Ab, with relief, moves to the ram.

(26) As ram speaks he should free himself from the bush and race across the stage. It is not possible to give exact moves for this, they must be worked out as you go, making sure that there is no masking, that all can be heard, that facial expressions can be seen, and that an atmosphere of panic is created! It is vital that the ram is extremely 'over the top', as the comedy comes from the echoing of the more serious dialogue repeated twice before, between God and Ab, and Ab and Isaac.

Isaac	*(Jumping off the fire, very relieved)* Yes! **(27)**
Chorus D	NO! *(Pleading)*
Isaac	YES! *(Triumphantly)* **(28)**
Chorus D	NO! *(Trying to escape)*
Ab	YES! *(Puts him firmly on the altar)*
Chorus D	*(With a sigh of resignation)* Oh, all right then.
Ab	*(Slits Ram's throat and all make a slitting throat action and appropriate noise)* **(29)**
Chorus C	And so the celebration began. **(30)**
Chorus B	They danced round the fire
Chorus D	*(Coming to life with a horrified expression)* And ate roast ram. **(31)**
Chorus A and C	The moral of this tale is that God will provide
Ab and Isaac	For all those who trust in him, and in his will abide. **(32)**

(All freeze)

(27)   Isaac throws off his chains, and must be expansive in movement showing his great relief. Ab hugs Isaac, and both momentarily glance up.

(28)   Isaac runs to ram, grabs it as nose to nose he says 'Yes'. Ram struggles as he is handed over to Ab, who fastens it on the altar. Ram, by this time has a very 'hangdog' expression. Chorus react at each turn of events, finally joyful at the outcome and moving at this time to new positions ready for the sacrificial dance! All freeze, just before laying the ram on the altar, thus focusing on the ram's line 'Oh, all right then'. This line should be delivered in a resentful and sulky acceptance, in direct contrast to the reactions of Ab and Isaac previously. The audience will identify with the ram, and so the faith of Ab will be recognised.

(29)   All turn to audience as Ab slits ram's throat, echoing Ab's action and making appropriate sounds, or just doing the old throat slit action!

(30)   All freeze for a second and then as Chorus C directly addresses the audience, they leap and dance around the altar. Think carefully about this staging, so that everyone knows exactly where they are at any given moment, remembering that the chorus must be able to address the audience easily on their lines, without slowing the action. If the group finds this difficult just freeze the action at a particular time of wild abandon! The ram dies spectacularly. That goes without being said!

(31)   Ram comes to life, to deliver this line, and *must not* be MASKED. (See *Foundation Workshop, Foundation Stone 10.*) After delivering the line with horror, it dies again sheepishly (I can't believe I wrote that!) Everyone else mimes grabbing bits of ram and eating voraciously for 2-3 seconds only.

(32)   All move as one *(including ram)* to final positions *before* delivering the line. I suggest that they all go back to the original positions held at the beginning, except that this time Ab looks heavenwards, and Isaac looks trustingly at Ab. Chorus focus actions on the two as before.

Eeeee-Aaaaaw! – Workshop

Luke 10:25-37

THEME

Love your enemy.

DURATION

3 hours 50 minutes to 4 hours. Easily split into two 2-hour sessions.

BUILDING MATERIALS

- Bible
- Tape recorder/cassette player
- Character cards
  (see list under 'Characterisation')
- A medium sized branch in a weighted plant pot or container.
- A blindfold for each member of the group
- Several small sheets of paper (a quarter A4 size) with hole punched in one corner.
- A tape recording of Colossians 3:12-17 (optional). A card with the text could be sufficient.

SPIRITUAL WARM-UP

5-10 minutes

PRAYER AND DEDICATION

Lord, we come together in fellowship to worship you through our drama offering. We pray for those who are living in sorrow and hatred, and ask that your healing love will be poured upon their situations. We ask help so that we may better understand other people regardless of race or creed, and love them as you love us. Help us to understand your word more clearly as we work together, and to see where it affects our own lives today. We ask you for the ability to communicate our ideas and feelings to each other as we work and explore your word. We dedicate this time to your glory. In the name of Jesus Christ our Lord, Amen.

CHORUS

Let there be love (88, *Easy-to-Play Choruses*, Kevin Mayhew Ltd; and 298, *Hymns Old &*

New, New Anglican Edition, Kevin Mayhew Ltd.)

PREPARING THE GROUND

10 minutes

BREATHING AND RELAXATION

Play a quiet piece of music during this exercise.

All to lie flat on backs in a space away from each other. It is important that they are relaxed with hands by sides, fingers unclenched, legs uncrossed and feet flopping outwards with eyes closed. Ask them to think through the events of the day, and imagine that they have a suitcase into which they can fold them and put them away.

Foundation Stone 1

We often find ourselves in situations where we are afraid to offer the hand of friendship, through prejudice, ignorance, fear, sheer laziness, or because we are too busy to notice. Bring to mind a time when we have turned away from helping someone. Quietly offer the situation to God, and ask forgiveness for our lack of action.

Then they must imagine that the lid on the suitcase is shut and their minds uncluttered, and ready to begin the workshop. Breathe in as deeply as possible, through the nose. (Asthma sufferers may find this hard, so adapt.) Then let the breath go out through the mouth. Do this five times. Get them to put their hands on their diaphragm and feel the lungs expanding the rib cage, and imagine that a magnet is making them feel incredibly heavy as it pulls them through the floor – they cannot move as all their body is heavy.

Ask them to stretch taut only their hands and then relax them, work through the body isolating as far as possible each set of muscles, stretching and relaxing them. Hands, hands and arms, feet, feet and legs, stomach muscles, shoulders, chest, neck, and finally all face muscles (open eyes and mouth wide, stretch tongue, etc.).

Finally stretch the whole body and relax, twice. Slowly sit up.

Foundation Stone 2

It is worth spending time on the initial part of this exercise. Emphasise the body and voice as instruments of communication. Explain how voice is produced through vocal chords, and pressure of breath. Explain how important it is to be able to control the voice, facial expressions and body shape when communicating through drama. Emphasise self-control and self-discipline. Parallel with training in sports or music, etc. It takes practice!

VOICE WARM-UP

10 minutes

A-E-I-O-U

Lie in a space on the floor.

Bring knees up so that feet are flat on the floor.

Take a deep breath (as in breathing and relaxation) and softly sing any note to the sound of ay, taking more breaths where necessary, controlling the output of breath as long as possible and changing to ee, then iy, oh and oo.

Finally, using the change of sounds in own time, *chew* on the sounds and spit them out. Notice what happens to the sound as the shape of the mouth changes, and as the amount of breath increases and decreases.

Chewy toffee tongue-twister

In a circle, leader joining in, imagine that you have a very large piece of toffee in your mouth. Chew it, stretching jaws, etc. This will cause great amusement at first, but encourage self-control!

Stick tongue out as far as possible (much dribbling here – be prepared) and touch chin, nose, then right cheek, followed by left cheek. Repeat several times.

If they are getting the hang of this, get them to learn and recite the following tongue twister, firstly with tongues out, then normally. If you feel really adventurous, get them to repeat it angrily, joyfully, sarcastically, etc.

How much wood would a woodchuck chuck
If a woodchuck could chuck wood?
A woodchuck would chuck everything he could chuck
If a woodchuck could chuck wood!

Foundation Stone 3

After the dribbles have been wiped away, ask them to tell you how different the inside of their mouth feels. Answer: aching, larger, stretched. If they don't feel this way, then they need to stretch even more.

Now repeat the following words with tongue stuck out as far as possible. Try to keep the words as clear as possible. Repeat again normally, but using your mouth in an exaggerated way.

Father Abraham has many sons.
Many sons has Father Abraham.
I am one of them and so are you.
So let's all praise the Lord!

Teach the tune of Father Abraham. (See *Glossary*.)

Foundation Stone 4

Emphasise clear diction.

WORK IN PAIRS

25 minutes

Head-to-head

In twos, sit on the floor facing each other, making sure that each couple is in their own private space. Give them one minute each on each theme. If they don't finish, tell them to find time to get together on their own and complete the discussion.

Themes:
Tell your partner about someone you dislike, and why.
Tell about a time when you needed comfort or help, and what happened. How did you feel?

Foundation Stone 5

We are all dependent upon one another at some time. People must be able to trust us, and we must be able to trust others. Sometimes a life may depend on this, you never know. We must learn to be responsible for each other, to care and support, to be there when needed. It is a lonely world when we are afraid and have no friends to help us through.

BLIND TRUST

Everyone into a space on their own, and put on blindfolds. Turn around five times to the left and five times to the right. Imagine that you are afraid and alone, and that you don't want to have contact with anyone. You have been hurt, and are afraid that it may happen again.

Move around the space avoiding contact with each other at all costs. Tell them that you are there to see that they do not bump into walls or chairs.

Don't let it continue for longer than two or three minutes. No speaking or sounds allowed. They must listen for others and avoid any contact. Then stop them.

Ask them to imagine that someone wants to be their friend and help them, then move around again, aiming for contact. Get them to join hands with another person. When both hands are held, they must stand still, otherwise follow where they are taken. As leader, you will have to guide those who are totally lost, until they have joined hands with someone. They will usually finish in circles, even one big circle, but they will be joined.

Now read or play a tape of Colossians 3:12-17. This should take about four minutes.

Without removing the blindfolds or speaking to each other get them to turn to the person on their left and using the sense of touch, try to work out who it is. Emphasise no talking or laughing.

Take off the blindfolds and let them see if they were correct.

DISCUSSION

All sit in a circle and share feelings about each experience.

Foundation Stone 6

We feel safer when we are held up by each other. The parallel is that God himself, through Christ, offers us his hand at all times, and especially when we are in need.

WORK IN GROUPS

50 minutes

ESSENCE MACHINES 1

Remember the Essence Machines in 'Surveying the Ground' Foundation Workshop? Exactly the same but with different themes! Here's a reminder:

Divide them into groups of no more than five and no less than three. Ask how they can tell the difference between different ice-creams or drinks. Introduce the word 'essence' and draw the parallel between types of ice-cream and different themes or types of scene in a play. Show an example.

Foundation Stone 7

Use one group to demonstrate an 'essence machine' with the theme 'Friends'. Firstly, stand them in a line and ask them to think of a word, phrase or activity to describe 'Friends'. For example:

- *'My best friend is . . .'*
- *'A friend in need is a friend indeed.'*
- *'It's lonely without a friend.'*
- *'My friend's better than your friend, so there!'*

These sentences do not have to be related. Run it through in order, repeating it over and over like a machine. Secondly, ask them to think of an action to go with their phrase. Now run that through in order. Ask the rest how the demonstrators could make it more interesting to watch.

Get them to refer back to LEVELS, MASKING, ACCURATE MIME, etc. Encourage the rest to direct the changes, until the sequence is easily recognisable. (See Surveying the Ground – Foundation Workshop.)

Give each group a card with a theme on it. They must use the same procedure to get to the essence of the idea, and create a machine as demonstrated. Time restricted to 10 minutes maximum.

Themes:
    Hatred
    Friendship
    Fear
    Compassion

Each group is given a different theme. Don't tell the others what it is. Try to guess during the Sharing.

SHARING

Watch and comment positively on the machines. Levels, visual appearance, volume and content to be considered. Encourage positive comments from the group.

QUICK PICS AND STORY BOARDING

15-20 minutes

Read the parable of the Good Samaritan (Luke 10:25-37). Discuss in small groups of three or four, the main points of the story (listed below). Give each group two cards with an aspect of the story, and the Bible reference. Ask each group to prepare a TABLEAU or a QUICK PIC which communicates that aspect.

- Jew on journey (lonely rocky road with an odd bush?)
- Attacked by robbers (part way through beating).
- Priest nervously 'passing by'.
- Levite deliberately ignoring cries for help.
- Samaritan assisting and binding up wounds.
- Samaritans and Jews – tableau of general enmity.
- Arrival at the inn – innkeeper's surprise.
- Grateful thanks.

A *Quick Pic* reminder is useful here: Give them 15 seconds to create a visual image of the main points of the story. (Leader counts down the seconds.) On the count of fifteen the command 'freeze' is given, and the leader gives points to the best three. Encourage them to use LEVELS and imaginative body shapes, discourage straight lines.

Foundation Stone 8

Emphasise the need to pick out the main points of the story, in as simple a way as possible, cutting out any unnecessary words, and concentrating on the meaning and message as well as the story. This should bridge into the present day.

SHARING AND DISCUSSION

Show the story board pics in order and pick out together the good points and ways of improvement. Read the verses as they freeze in position.

ESSENCE MACHINES 2

Each group to make an essence machine of the message and content of the Good Samaritan, using the main points of the story listed.

Divide them into groups of no more than five and no less than three, and remind them of the essences presented earlier, drawing the parallel again between types of ice-cream and different themes or types of scene in a play. Show an example here, from those prepared earlier, if you feel it would help.

Give each group a card with a main point of the story on it. They must use the same procedure to get to the essence of the idea, and create a machine as demonstrated. Time restricted to 15 minutes maximum, less if possible!

BUILDING INSPECTION

- Discuss positives.
- Discuss possible improvements.

Foundation Stone 9

Always encourage the group to be positive and constructive in their criticisms, so go for the good things first. Then look at the negative things under the umbrella of possible improvements. This is a much less threatening way of dealing with presentations. 'It's not what you say, it's the way that you say it!'

You will probably find that the group tends to be negative in their criticism at first. Don't allow it. Make them use the terminology you require.

Encourage truthful comment at all times. If someone is deliberately fooling about, which often happens, tell them in no uncertain terms that they are being destructive, but try to assess why they are behaving this way before you wade in too heavily, for giggles and laughter often are signs of embarrassment and nerves.

Consider the following:
- *Can it be heard?*
- *Is the visual communication accurate?*
- *Is the mime believable?*
- *Are the group really concentrating?*
- *Are they making the best use of levels?*
- *Is there evidence of good group co-operation?*
- *Stress – Be critical without being unkind. Positive and constructive not negative and destructive. All offerings are valuable.*
- *Remember – Everyone has something to offer, and something to learn.*

WHOLE GROUP WORK

60-80 minutes

CHARACTERISATION – STEREOTYPES

Levite, Priest, Vicar, Scholar, Chinese person, Alien, Robber, Yob, Polite gentleman, Tramp, Policeman, Old person, Spoiled child, Politician, Children's TV presenter.

Prior to the workshop, make character cards from the resource list above, making sure that there is one for each member of the group. Number them on the reverse side. Place them, number side up all around the working area.

Ask the group to move into a space. On a given signal (a drum beat is effective), the group move around the space, changing direction on command and on hearing a double drum beat they stop and pick up a character card, read it, think about the character, age, looks, attitude, clothing, voice, way of walking, etc.

and put the card back on the floor, face down. Then they make a frozen statue of the character.

On the next signal, they are to move as the character, paying attention to the personality and age, occupation and attitude of the character on their card.

On the next signal, they freeze and listen to the following instructions. Imagine that your character has a sound, *not* words, just a sound. It may be high, low, smooth, aggressive, frightened, cheeky, bossy or whatever – use your imagination!

Then again, on the signal, they move 'IN CHARACTER' and add the sound of their personality. Stop them again and ask them to imagine their character in a normal situation such as buying a newspaper, asking to see a menu, or talking to a friend.

They must then imagine what their character might be thinking or saying in that situation. On the next signal they move and speak the thoughts of that character out loud. This is called a THOUGHT TRACK. They must block out other people, and concentrate on the voice, mannerisms, walk and, most of all, FEELINGS, of their character. All do this together, as it avoids embarrassment for the shy members of the group.

Finally FREEZE them again and ask them to turn to the nearest person and have a conversation with them, again, keeping in character.

If the group is confident enough you can explain that you are going to freeze them again and ask them to continue their conversation when you tap one of them on the shoulder. Let each couple have a go, but if anyone is too nervous, or hasn't much to say, just freeze them again and go on to the next pair.

Foundation Stone 10

Emphasise keeping 'in character' all the time. Don't be distracted by others. If everyone concentrates on their own work then no one is being watched. Remember voice, posture, attitude, etc. Tell them that we all are inclined to stereotype people, as the Jews stereotype the Samaritans and vice versa. Do policemen always say "'ello, 'ello, 'ello"?

DISCUSSION

Discuss together things which were good about individuals or pairs, and ways in which their interpretation could be improved. Discourage laughter which is out of character. Think about tone of voice, accent, diction and whether individuals were able to keep in character at all times. Discuss how any problems might be overcome.

CHARACTERISATION – PERSONALITY PROFILE

Give out a piece of paper and a pencil to each member of the group and ask them to choose a character from the story of the good Samaritan. Alternatively you can give them a paper with the character written on it, and make them focus on that. It sometimes saves time with less experienced group members to do it that way. The choice is yours.

Now sit them in a space alone, and with *no collaboration*, ask them to jot down their ideas. If you want to be more structured, you can pose some or all of the following questions:

- Age? Height?
- Hair colour, clothing, place they come from, family?
- Where are they going in the story?
- Where have they come from?
- What is their purpose in life?
- What is their favourite occupation?
- What annoys them most?

I'm sure you can think of more of these. You will need to help some people by moving around the group answering questions.

Foundation Stone 11

All characters and people have much more to them than just their outward image and appearance. So explain that the group is going to think about the characters in the story, and develop them into people with a background, family, purpose in life and so on.

HEAD-TO-HEAD

Reminder: In pairs, sit facing each other in a space, close enough to be heard when speaking quietly and far enough away from others to hold a private conversation. In one minute (timed carefully) tell as much as possible on each theme.

Decide who is A and who is B and take it in turns to have one minute's speaking time. Change partners for each theme. In twos let them tell each other about their characters, swap ideas and add more details.

Foundation Stone 12

It may be necessary here to input some information about the period in which the story was written, such as the customs and attitudes at the time. This is where the Bible teaching for a purpose comes in! The hatred of the Jews for the Samaritans should be covered, plus a little about journeys and their purpose. E.g. Why was the Samaritan travelling that day? Why might the Jew have been alone in obviously dangerous territory? Who were the robbers and bandits?

IMPROVISATION

In groups of four or five, improvise the story of the Good Samaritan, with a cast of Jew, Samaritan, Robbers, Priest, Levite, hotel owner. To save time, you could divide the story into sections and give each group one section only. However, it is better if they can all experience the whole story! Put a time limit on the length of the scene of 5 minutes, otherwise you could be there all night!

Foundation Stone 13

The first complaint will be 'we haven't enough in our group to do the story!' Refer them back to essence machines and story boarding, and suggest that some people can play more than one character.

There could be problems in the starting of each scene, so remind them of STORY BOARDING and suggest that they can do each scene by bringing tableaux to life. Stress that it is possible to be on stage and yet not involved in the dialogue, by using the NEUTRAL idea. They can turn their backs to the audience in 'neutral' (see Glossary), and on a given cue, can become another character. Neutral involves standing still and relaxed, with feet slightly apart, to give good balance.

They must mime everything, and can be anything, from a door to the inn, to a bush! Remind them of QUICK PICS.

Emphasise staying 'in character' too. You never know, what they produce, with editing and polishing, could be good enough to perform in its own right!

SHARING AND BUILDING INSPECTION

- Watch each scene.
- Discuss the positives first.

Ask the following questions and discuss together:
- Could you hear everyone?
- Did everyone stay in character?
- What was the scene like visually?
- What message(s) came across.
- What was really good about each scene?
- How could it be adapted to fit in your acting area ?
- What does the story mean to us today? (For further ideas, see Foundation Workshop – Foundation Stones 12 and 13)

OPTIONAL STORY

This story simply re-emphasises how we can all find ourselves in situations where we walk by on the other side, when we should instead kneel down and help, like the Samaritan.

One of the original Mustard Seeds, who lives in London, was walking through Leicester Square, at a very busy time, when it was buzzing with tourists, theatre-goers, shoppers and cinema-goers. As she walked along she saw a man in the middle of the square, lying on the ground, obviously either in great need, or in a coma, or full of drugs. Everyone pretended not to see, and walked around and even over the body, too scared or disinterested to do anything about it. There are so many needy and homeless in London.

She too found herself avoiding the body and walking on. But after a few steps, she suddenly stopped in her tracks. 'What am I doing?' she thought. 'I'm supposed to be a Christian, I know the story of the Samaritan, and yet I behaved like the person passing by on the other side.' She was horrified at what she had done, and knew that she must put things right. But how? He could have a knife, he might attack her. He might be dead. What would people think?

She couldn't turn away, and being a sensible girl, called on someone to help. 'We can't just leave him there. Phone for an ambulance,' she said. It only took one person, and then a small crowd gathered to see what was happening, someone got an ambulance, and the man was carried away.

The thought that she might have joined the worldly attitude and left him there, has haunted her ever since. She was so glad that God had tapped her on the shoulder and reminded her of the Samaritan and the Jew. She resolved to be more aware in future. As should we all!

CLOSING ACTIVITY AND PRAYER

10-15 minutes

Give out a small piece of paper and a pencil to everyone as they sit in a circle. Ask them to write down an area or situation in the world, or within their family where reconciliation and love could make the difference. As they write, place the branch which you prepared beforehand in a pot in the centre of the circle. This is the prayer tree. When all are ready, put the prayers in a hat and let everyone pick one out. Read out the prayers in the circle and offer each one to God. After each prayer is finished, the person reading it hangs it on to the prayer tree.

CHORUS

Jesus stand among us. (77, *Easy-To-Play Choruses*, Kevin Mayhew Ltd; 279, *Hymns Old & New*, New Anglican Edition, Kevin Mayhew Ltd.)

CLOSING PRAYER

We thank you for our time together, and ask that we may go out into our lives in the strength of your Spirit, to love and serve our fellow human beings, whoever they may be, wherever we may find them, at whatever risk to ourselves. Help us to be Samaritans in a world of hatred and prejudice.

The Lord's Prayer

The Grace

(Together, eyes open, making contact with each other. Holding hands is a good way of doing this.)

Eeeeee-Aaaaaw! – A Sketch
Luke 10:25-37. The parable of the Good Samaritan.

Characters: Levite, Jew, Samaritan

(All begin with backs to audience) **(1)**

All	*(Turn)* Once, *(slight pause)* there was a man **(2)**
Levite	Who went on a journey
Jew	From Jerusalem *(All point SR)* **(3)**
Samaritan	To Jericho. *(All point SL, then turn, walking on the spot)*
Levite	When he fell *(Turn head to audience, still walking)*
Jew	*(Scared, turning head to audience)* Into the hands **(4)**
Samaritan	*(To audience)* Of robbers. **(5)**
Jew	*(Screams. Levite and Sam tower above him)* Aaaaaaaargh! *(falls into Levite's arms)* **(6)**
Samaritan	They stripped him *(Levite and Samaritan two mime stripping Jew)* **(7)**
Jew	Oh! *(covers himself)*
Samaritan	*(Conversationally)* Beat him! *(Levite knees Jew)* **(8)**
Jew	Ow!
Samaritan	Ugh! *(Thumps Jew)*
Jew	*(CS)* Aaargh!
Sam and Levite	Ugh! *(Put feet on Jew with victory shouts)* **(9)**
Levite	*(As Narrator, to Samaritan)* Then
Samaritan	*(As Narrator, to Levite)* They went on their way.

Director's Tips

(1) Positioning at the beginning of this sketch is important, because of following action. Therefore Jew is Centre, Levite on his right *(SR)*, and Samaritan on his left *(SL)*. They should all face upstage standing in neutral (See *Surveying the Ground – Foundation Workshop, Foundation Stone 4*).

(2) They must be sensitive to each other and turn at exactly the same time and in the same direction, e.g. with right shoulder leading *(or left if that is easier)*. You can get them to turn as they take a breath to speak. (See *Ab and Isaac,* MIME WALK) Also diction and clarity of speech are vital when speaking together. THERE IS NOTHING WORSE THAN SLURRED ENDINGS OR OVERLAPPING WORDS *(unless for a specific purpose!)*

(3) Speak the lines as if selling a product on a TV advert, then immediately on the cue Jericho, turn to the left, and begin to walk on the spot. (See *Ab and Isaac Workshop,* MIME WALK.)

(4) All turn and walk on the spot. Levite addresses audience, then looks ahead again. Jew does the same, but gestures with hands on that word. Levite uses the same cue and the same hand gesture.

(5) Similarly Samaritan addresses the audience and then turns to face Levite over the head of Jew, and immediately into 'threatening position'. Often in this sketch, the actors tell the story through a variety of different characters, in this sort of way. Similarly Jew shrinking between them becomes the frightened victim and screams. Levite becomes another threatening robber. These things happen with great pace and need careful rehearsal to keep it going at speed.

(6) As Jew screams he/she falls backwards into the arms of Levite. (See *Eeee-Aaaaaw and Ab and Isaac Workshops, Trust and Blind Trust.*)

(7) 'Stripping' must be done in one movement. I suggest that Samaritan and Levite bob down with a downward hand and arm movement, coinciding with Jew 'covering' movement and look of horror.

(8) Levite knees Jew *(in mime of course!)* Remember that whenever there is an ACTION, there is always a REACTION. Similarly Samaritan, holding both hands together, 'chops' him at the back of the neck, and he falls to the floor as he screams.

(9) Upstage legs rest on Jew – downstage arms raised, fists clenched. A momentary freeze before looking at each other. Noise they make must be short but Yob-like!

Levite and Samaritan	Bye! (*Both wave, Samaritan SL, Levite SR and moves SR*) **(10)**
Levite	(*Cheerfully*) Leaving him
Jew	(*Cheerfully*) Half dead. (*Both back to Jew, viciously kick him, laugh and move back to USR [Samaritan] and SL [Levite]*) **(11)**
Levite	A priest was walking by.
Samaritan	(*In character of Priest, moves CS behind Jew*) A-a-men! **(12)**
Jew	Argghh! (*Groan*)
Levite	And saw the man. (*Pause, watch action for a moment, then move USR in neutral with back to audience*) **(13)**
Jew	(*Groaning, with hand stretched out for help*) Help!
Samaritan	(*deliberately keeps at a distance*) Are you injured? (*Politely*) Are you bleeding? **(14)**
Jew	Help! (*Weaker cry*)
Samaritan	(*Deliberately hovering far away*) Excuse me! Are you hurt? Who did this to you?
Jew	(*Weakly*) Robbers!
Samaritan	(*As priest, horrified, looks around fearfully*) Robbers! (*Obvious excuse*) Must be on my way. I'm late for prayers. A-a-men. (*Hurriedly moves DSR*) **(15)** (*Turn as Narrator*) A man of the law was also passing by (*Levite mutters as he reads, and walks towards Jew*) **(16)**
Samaritan	He fell over the injured man. (*Levite trips over the body*)
Levite	(*Irritated and turning pages of the Torah*) I've lost my page! (*Finds page*) Oh! There we are! (*Turns, relieved, moves SL*) **(17)**
Samaritan	And went on his way. (*Moves USR back to audience in neutral.*)

(10) Move away again, turn and wave, using mainly fingers, like a silly child who thinks he's funny, and with a smirking smile. 'Leaving him' is spoken as they walk a couple of steps DSR and DSL.

(11) On 'half dead', they turn, move swiftly back to Jew, mime another vicious kick in unison and with great enthusiasm before moving to new positions.

(12) Singing as in a chant. Hands together in prayer, pious expression.

(13) Hold the pause until the word 'Are' is spoken by the Samaritan, then turn with back to audience in neutral. (See *Surveying the Ground, Foundation Workshop, Foundation Stone 4*.)

(14) In character of priest, sounds kind but deliberately hovering at a distance, with occasional nervous glances about, in case the robbers should return. Much of this is communicated by body language (see *In the Bag Workshop, and Handshake Hullaballoo*).

(15) This move must be quick, but in character. He must end the move in neutral, with back to the audience, hold neutral for a second, then turn as Narrator.

(16) As Samaritan turns to audience, Levite comes to life, a rather wizened, hunch-shouldered person, walking with small hurried steps. Rather shortsightedly turning the pages of the Torah, he mutters, as if reading aloud.

(17) Levite must mutter and keep in character all the way. Ideally he should not even stop as he trips over the body. The 'trip' must be rehearsed until it looks quite natural.

Levite	(*As Narrator*) A Samaritan
Samaritan	(*Turns, becomes Samaritan leading imaginary donkey*) Eeee-aw. **(18)**
Levite	And his donkey were on a journey.
Samaritan	(*leads donkey, sees body*) A JEW! **(19)**
Jew	(*Even more horrified*) A Samaritan!
Levite	The Jews and Samaritans were great enemies.
Jew	(*Terrified, raises hands to protect himself*) Don't hurt me. **(20)**
Samaritan	(*Kneels. Speaks compassionately.*) You are injured. You are bleeding. Please let me help you. (*Mimes actions during next speeches*) **(21)**
Levite	The Samaritan poured wine and oil on the Jew's injuries and bandaged them up. He then placed him on his donkey.
Samaritan	Hey! where's my donkey? (*Beckons him*) You'll do! **(22)**
Levite	(*Becomes donkey, the Jew his passenger*) **(23)**
Samaritan	(*As Narrator*) Then the Samaritan took the Jew to the nearest inn. (*Picks up Jew and knocks on imaginary door SR. Levite runs in front of Samaritan and becomes innkeeper and opens door.*)
Samaritan	(*Cheerfully*) Hello! **(24)**
Levite	(*Gasp, looking in horror at him*)
Samaritan	I have an injured man for you.
Levite	(*Shocked expression*) But he's a Jew . . . and you're a Samaritan! **(25)**
Samaritan	Please, will you take care of him? (*gives Jew to Levite*) Here is some money. I'll visit you tomorrow. (*All form a line facing the audience*) **(26)**
Jew	Jesus asked, 'which of the three men showed mercy to his neighbour?' (*Pause*) The priest? **(27)**

(18)   Turn on Samaritan, briskly, taking on the character immediately, perhaps some business with the imaginary donkey could emerge here? A refusal to move, and encouragement, etc. Just briefly!

(19)   Leads donkey DSC to Jew – we *must* believe in the donkey, and we must believe that the injured man looks terribly wounded, so Samaritan's reaction to the body is vital. Facial expression very important. He could step back slightly and point as he questions 'A Jew', although his hairstyle would probably give him away.

(20)   Use body language, to show fear of being beaten up again, protecting face with hands, or as if fending off an attacker.

(21)   He mimes the actions told by the narrator. Don't rush them, even if the narrator finishes before the Samaritan has bandaged the Jew. This is the crux of the whole piece, that you should show compassion for your enemies, and is the serious part of the sketch, contrasting with the lighthearted approach in the rest of it. Don't aim for the longest Oscar-winning performance though – but *make it real*. (See *In the Bag Workshop, Catch that Cue*.)

(22)   Samaritan looks around for the donkey, an edge of panic in his voice. Perhaps the robbers have taken it while he was so busy! Catches the eye of Levite who reads his mind, facial expression here. Rather enjoying the idea, he beckons Levite with a mischievous grin. Levite resentfully joins him, letting the audience see his thoughts on the matter!

(23)   How does Levite become a donkey you ask? Well, he turns to face the direction in which he is to walk, leans forward from the waist, then Jew comes up behind him, in the same position and leans on him, with face towards audience. Then walking in step, together they move to the new position as 'donkey' and passenger!

(24)   As donkey and passenger reach SR, the Levite moves behind the Samaritan to SR, turns and faces left. The Samaritan knocks on an imaginary door, turns and picks up Jew in his arms. Then Levite opens the door, and 'Hello' is spoken. Again it must be slick and well rehearsed.

(25)   All the shock and horror of someone who knows how much Jews and Samaritans hate each other must be heard in the voice, and seen on the face. Melodramatic (*Mildly!*).

(26)   Levite carries Jew, and the Samaritan gives him money. On the cue 'tomorrow', Jew is put down on R of Levite and, Samaritan on his left, they turn to audience.

(27)   Cue 'Priest', Samaritan takes up Priest's posture, with praying hands as he sings 'Amen'.

Samaritan	A-a-men. **(28)**
Jew	The man of the law?
Levite	*(In character of Levite, reading, annoyed)* I've lost my page!
Jew	Or the Samaritan?
Samaritan	Let me help you!
Levite	*(As donkey)* Eeee-aw.
Jew	*(Smiling fondly)* And his donkey. **(29)**
Samaritan	The priest walked by on the other side.
Levite	As did the man of the law.
Jew	But the Samaritan showed mercy, even unto his enemy. Jesus said,
All	Go, *(Pause)* and do the same. **(30)**
Levite	Eeee-aw.
All	Eeeee-aw. *(Exit)* **(31)**

(28)   On the 'men' of 'A-a-men', Levite takes up the stance of Levite reading his book. On the cue 'page' Samaritan speaks directly to the audience, as Samaritan. Levite cannot restrain himself and brays as donkey. Samaritan and Jew look at him fondly, Levite slightly embarrassed.

(29)   Next speeches are as Narrator.

(30)   Choral speech, keep together, begin and end words. Eye contact with audience so that they are clear that the message is for all present!

(31)   A little comic relief to sweeten the serious message, then all three turn and exit, making sure that the exit is in unison!

In the Bag – Workshop
Matthew 13:1-9 and 18-22

THEME

Hearing God's Word and acting upon it.

Duration

2¹/₂ hours to 4¹/₂ hours.

Building Materials

- Bible
- Tape recorder/cassette player
- CD or tape with a good beat
- Three soft balls or three bean bags

SPIRITUAL WARM-UP

10 minutes

Prayer and Dedication

Heavenly Father, we ask that our time together will be fruitful, with abundant ideas, and greater understanding of your word. Help us to grow closer together in an atmosphere of harmony, that we may not allow distractions from outside in our lives, or inside where we are working, to divert us from learning more about the way we should respond to your love. We dedicate this time to your glory, and offer our work and ourselves to you, for it is from you that all our gifts come. In the name of Jesus Christ, Amen.

Chorus

I am a new creation (49, *Easy-to-Play Choruses*, Kevin Mayhew Ltd; 221, *Hymns Old & New*, New Anglican Edition, Kevin Mayhew Ltd.)

PREPARING THE GROUND

10 minutes

Breathing and Relaxation

Play a quiet piece of music during this exercise. All to lie flat on backs in a space away from each other. It is important that they are relaxed with hands by sides, fingers unclenched, legs uncrossed and feet flopping outwards and their eyes closed.

Ask them to think through the events of the day, and imagine that they have a suitcase into which they can fold them and put them away. Then they must imagine that the lid on the suitcase is shut and their minds uncluttered, and ready to begin the workshop.

Breathe in as deeply as possible, through the nose. (Asthma sufferers may find this hard, so adapt.) Then let the breath go out through the mouth. Do this five times. Get them to put their hands on their diaphragm and feel the lungs expanding the rib cage.

Get them to imagine that a magnet is making them feel incredibly heavy as it pulls them through the floor. They cannot move as all their body is heavy.

Stretch taut (hands only) and then relax them, work through the body isolating as far as possible each set of muscles, stretching and relaxing them. Hands, hands and arms, feet, feet and legs, stomach muscles, shoulders, chest, neck, and finally face muscles (open eyes and mouth wide, stretch tongue, etc.).

Finally stretch the whole body and relax, twice. Slowly sit up.

Shake out

All stand in a space.

Using a popular CD or cassette with a good medium to fast rhythm, shake out hands, arms legs, hips, face. Finish by moving in any way to the rhythm. Shake right hand, then left hand, feet, hips, shoulders, heads and whole body in time to the music. Stretch high, touch toes (Mr. Motivator's got nothing on this!) at least ten times.

Roll head round slowly to the left in a full circle, then to the right. Repeat five times each.

Slowly, vertebra by vertebra (beginning with the base of the neck and working down), bend from the waist. Then swing arms to the right and to the left five times each, finally slowly uncurl to standing position, vertebra by vertebra, beginning at the base of the spine.

Move into a circle, and each member of the group devises a simple (but energetic, please) movement which is copied by the others. You can add to this by making it mobile. Move around the room, copying the leader, who keeps changing the moves.

Foundation Stone 1

Encourage the more athletic to temper their moves so that all can join in, and adapt for the disabled accordingly. But don't let laziness creep in! (No slugs allowed!)

GROUP UNITY

5 minutes

GROUP YELL

All move out to the edges of the room, and crouch low on the ground. Sing 'Aaah' on any note very softly and gradually, as a group, following each other, building to a crescendo. As the sound builds slowly, so the members of the group slowly, as one person, rise to their feet and move to the centre.

When they reach the centre of the circle the volume should build to its loudest, culminating in a word which is shouted at full volume as the group jumps as one person with hands stretched in the air. A word relevant to the theme can be chosen. However, the following have been known to go down well: sausages, the name of a favourite pop band, Amen, and in this case 'In the Bag' could be appropriate. There will be many other suggestions, some of which will definitely have to be censored! This is a good game for drawing the group together, very simple, but they seem to enjoy it.

Foundation Stone 2

In order to work together effectively, we must be aware of others, and sensitive to them. It is always tempting for natural leaders to force the pace – don't. Allow the whole group to build up a momentum by using peripheral vision and keeping together, not only vocally, but physically

too. The bigger and faster people must slow down for the smaller and slower people, who in turn must push themselves to keep up. (There's a lesson in that somewhere!)

WORK IN PAIRS

30-40 minutes

MIRROR REFLECTIONS

Stand in twos in a space, facing each other, and decide who is A and who is B. When the music begins the A's start a movement and the B's follow the movement, as if in a mirror. After a short time change over. This must all be done in slow motion (Chariots of Fire style!). The aim is not to be able to tell who is leading.

The theme can be abstract, but if this is the first time they have done this, I would tend to be more prescriptive. Here are some ideas:

- A clown putting on make-up.
- Getting washed.
- Cleaning teeth.
- A puppet dancing.
- An artist painting a picture.

Foundation Stone 3

Try to look each other in the eyes while doing mirror reflection. Make movements very slow or the partner can't follow.

Make sure that any mime is accurate – like taking the lid off the toothpaste, and not letting things change size.

Be aware of your partner and don't do movements which they would be unable to do at the best of times.

BODY SHAPES – HANDSHAKE PHYSICAL IMPROVISATION

Change partners. (It's a good idea to avoid the same people always working together, and it gets the group integrated and knowing everyone well. Decide who is A and who is B. Shake hands.

When the leader bangs a drum, or gives a signal the two break hands, and A moves instantly and quickly into another shape in relation to B. Another drum beat and B changes shape again in relation to A. Once the shape and position have been changed there must be a total 'freeze'.

The shapes they make can involve linking and touching, but could equally well be unrelated. The important thing is to move without thinking and be as adventurous as possible.

Foundation Stone 4

It is important that they get rid of all embarrassment, and just enjoy the physicality of this. Never use the same position twice, always do something different. Remind them of levels. Encourage twisted and unusual body shapes, as this will be very useful in the sketch, as well as releasing inhibitions!

Stress the need to remain still, even if your partner is physically linked to you.

HANDSHAKE HULLABALLOO

Repeat Handshake improvisation, and when the shapes look really interesting and strange, freeze everyone, and tell them to improvise a conversation. They can be anyone and anywhere which their related shapes suggest. Let them all improvise together a couple of times.

Then choose particular couples to improvise on their own, immediately after the changing shapes routine. No time to think, just do it!

Foundation Stone 5

Encourage strange characters, situations, places, voices. Remind them that they can be anyone or anything, anywhere!

VOICE WARM-UP

20 minutes

CHEWY TOFFEE

In a circle, leader joining in, imagine that you have a very large piece of toffee in your mouth.

Chew it, stretching jaws, etc. This will cause great amusement at first, but encourage self-control!

Stick tongue out as far as possible and try to touch chin, nose, then right cheek, followed by left cheek. Repeat several times.

Now say the following with tongue stretched out:

> Peter Piper picked a peck of pickled pepper.
> If Peter Piper picked a peck of pickled
>   pepper,
> where's the peck of pickled pepper,
> Peter Piper picked?

Still with tongue out, say it:
- as if to a baby sitting in the centre of the circle
- angrily
- as if you are bored.

Repeat again (with tongue in this time) emphasising the mood *without* losing the beginnings and ends of words. Clear diction required. Speed it up as fast as you can to finish.

Foundation Stone 6

Emphasise the need for clear speech and good diction.

CAULIFLOWER

Sit in a circle, with the centre as the acting area. Prepare situation cards beforehand on the following themes:
- Invite everyone to a party
- Explain that a famous pop group (choose own group) are outside, and want to come in
- Persuade everyone that you are starving and that they must feed you or you will die!
- Tell everyone they must leave as there is a fire
- Describe how to plant a young tree
- Describe your favourite TV programme

The only rule is that you may only use the word 'cauliflower'! The rest of the circle have to try and guess what is being communicated. If they are unsuccessful then the 'actor' must try to communicate in a different way, come in on another angle, use different body language, improve mime and so on, to get the message across.

Foundation Stone 7

Emphasise the use of body language, tone of voice, facial expression, which is necessary to communicate. Stress its vital importance.

WORK IN GROUPS

50-60 minutes

Yes Yes Yes. No No No.

In groups of three (four will work if absolutely pushed) devise a short scene with the theme 'Danger, keep out'. The only words which can be used are 'yes' x 6 and 'no' once or 'No' x 6 and 'Yes' once. Share them and comment. Don't allow them to run longer than 1 minute each! (Unless you want to stay all night!)

Foundation Stone 8

No extra yes's or no's are allowed. The groups must convey the meaning of the scene through mime, facial expression, body language and tone of voice. If they have difficulty with this, get into a circle, and going round, experiment with as many tones of voice, etc., for each word, helping them, if necessary, by providing situations such as refusing to tidy your room, and not caring what happens, or someone offering you food you hate and you are being polite about refusing it.

Don't allow any muttering in the scenes, all the words must be heard clearly.

Encourage exaggerated body language, encourage laughter, it can always be calmed down later.

Old King Cole

50-60 minutes

All stand in a circle and chant 'Old King Cole wasa Merry old soul anda merry old soul wasa he.' This is repeated until all know it.

An action is then introduced on 'wasa', e.g. bending knees. Then repeat rhyme with all joining in the actions. Another simple action is introduced for 'anda', e.g. raising hands above heads.

Now the game begins. All take an individual word from the rhyme, in order, and speak it around the circle. As the rhyme goes around the circle, each person will speak a different word each time, unless of course you have a group of 13!

The person who gets the action words completes the action. If he fails he is 'out', and the game begins again, started by the person on the left of the one who was out, resuming at the beginning of the rhyme. Thus, whenever anyone is out, the whole procedure begins again. Also if anyone else in the circle uses the actions at the wrong time, they too are 'out'. The winners are the last three remaining.

Variation

Introduce another action for the word 'anda', i.e. knees bend, hands on knees. N.B. only the person saying 'anda' must do the action. Trial run until everyone knows the sequence and actions reasonably well.

Rules

Anyone who makes a mistake sits out. Anyone who hesitates sits out.

Emphasis

Clear diction, freedom of action, concentration, co-ordination.

Foundation Stone 9

Co-ordination is a vital skill which needs a great deal of practice. Diction and clear speech should be like second nature. When presenting anything, the actor must be aware of many things at the same time, and should be able to control body and voice at the same time. Aims: To develop concentration, encourage voice projection and clarity of diction in a game situation. Breathing/voice/concentration.

Now put everyone into groups of three or four, definitely no more than five. Give them the text of the Parable of the Sower to read and discuss. Make sure that they sit down in a circle to do this.

Ask them to work it out as a short series of scenes. The only restriction is that they may only say 'cauliflower' *or* 'yes' and 'no'.

SHARING

Share each scene together afterwards. Be positive about them, and discuss ways of improvement.

Foundation Stone 10

Characterisation, tone of voice and body language can tell a story without words. When you use words don't forget this experience. (See Foundation Stone 7 in the Ab and Isaac Workshop.)

WHOLE GROUP WORK

20 minutes

CATCH THAT CUE

Stand in a circle. The leader throws the ball to another member of the group, who passes it on, and so on until everyone has caught and thrown the ball. It finishes with the leader, and no one is allowed to catch the ball twice. Do this until a rhythm has been established.

Ask them to think of a category such as food, TV programmes, parables, football teams, etc. Each person thinks of, say, a kind of food, and when they throw the ball round, they call out the name of the food. This acts as a cue for the person who is catching. Keep going until there is a good rhythm going. Whenever there is a mistake, the ball goes back to the leader!

When this has been established, the leader takes another different coloured ball and chooses a different category. In this instance it could be phrases or words from the Sower, e.g. seeds, weeds, drought, rocky ground, etc. As this new ball is thrown, it cannot be passed to the same person you threw to in the first round.

Proceed as before, until there is a reasonable rhythm going. Then the leader adds the first category and both balls go round at the same time. When you get proficient you can add a third and a fourth category. But this takes time. It's a good game for sharpening concentration, eye contact, pace, and picking up on cues.

Foundation Stone 11

Emphasise the need to have eye contact with the person to whom you are throwing the ball.

Listen for your cues – never throw the ball to someone who is already in position, just alter the rhythm and wait to throw.

Project your voice, as others won't hear their cue unless you do. All this is like being in a sketch; you have to listen and respond to others at the right time, being sensitive to their needs.

Some people (there's always one isn't there?) will throw the ball deliberately hard so that it is dropped. Emphasise that this is a kind game and that the aim is to work as a team and enable everyone to play their part. Just like a play!

CLOSING PRAYER

5 minutes

Lord Jesus, We thank you for the opportunity to meet and explore your Word in this way. We thank you for the things which have borne fruit and the skills we have begun to learn. May this group provide good soil in which we can all grow in your light. Protect us from the worldly distractions and temptations which lure us away from the purity of your love. Help us to grow a hundredfold through the gentleness and power of your loving Spirit. Amen.

CHORUS

Abba, Father. (1, *Easy-to-Play Choruses*, Kevin Mayhew Ltd; 5, *Hymns Old & New*, New Anglican Edition, Kevin Mayhew Ltd.) Join hands as this is sung.

In the Bag – A Sketch
Matthew 13:1-9 and 18-23. The Parable of the Sower.

Characters: Acorn, Azalea, Chrysanthemum, Orchid

	(All characters stand in neutral with backs to the audience)
All	*(Turn)* Once . . . there was a farmer, who wanted to sow some seeds. **(1)**
	(All move swiftly into bag of seed positions) **(2)**
Acorn	Once there was a bag of seeds. **(3)**
All	*(High-pitched chatter)* **(4)**
Chrysanth	What are we going to do today?
Orchid	*(Slowly and ominously)* Out of the Bag. **(5)**
Acorn	Out of the Bag! *(looks up)* Oh-oh! **(6)**
Chrysanth	Oh-oh! *(Look towards audience and then back to 'hand')* **(6)**
Orchid	Oh-oh! *(Look towards audience and then back to 'hand')* **(6)**
Azalea	Oh-oh! *(Look towards audience and then back to 'hand')* **(6)**
Chrysanth	*(Horrified, looks up as if at giant hand and then looks at audience)* FINGERS! *(Screams, squeals of fear. Wriggle, struggle as if being picked up)* **(7)**
Acorn	It's gone up me nose! *(All leap out of 'Bag', Acorn to SL, Chrysanth to CS)* **(7)**
Azalea and Orchid	Ooooooooooh! *(leap and fall. Azalea DSR, Orchid SL. All groan and whimper, sit up and look around with interest as they rub various parts of their anatomy)* **(8)**
Azalea	Some of the seed fell on the path. *(With a surprised look.)*
Orchid	*(Wriggling in an uncomfortable way with a grimace)* It's a bit hard. **(9)**

Director's Tips

(1) NEUTRAL stance (See *'Surveying the Ground' Workshop, Foundation Stone 4*). The characters should be placed in an easy position for turning into the 'bag of seeds'. On the first turn they address the audience, using a narrative style, setting the mood for a story. Although this sketch works well for an adult audience, it was written with children in mind.

(2) This move into the 'bag' must be very quick; it happens several times in the sketch, and could be a serious 'slow up' of events if it is not slick and well rehearsed. It may be necessary to adjust the starting positions to create ease in this move. Once in position all freeze. Remember to make it look interesting, use levels, good facial expression, and interesting body shapes (see *'In The Bag' Workshop, Handshake Impro, Mirror Reflections*).

(3) Acorn's speech is most effective if his/her body stays still and the head only turns to address the audience. All the 'seeds' are also narrators, and must develop a 'storytelling' voice and a 'character' voice. It's useful to highlight the script accordingly, to remind the cast which is which!

(4) The chatter must sound non-human, and be in 'gobblydygook'. (See *'In the Bag' Workshop, Cauliflower, and Yes No games*) The length of time the chatter continues is important; don't let it go on longer than about 3-4 seconds.

(5) This is a catchphrase, but in this instance Orchid must use the lower register of the voice, and slow the line down sufficiently to create a sense of fear and apprehension amongst the seeds. Good diction vital.

(6) This section is repeated several times and should be a carbon copy each time. If I remember rightly the 'Oh-oh' was influenced by Dustin Hoffman in 'Rain Man' and should have a childlike quality to it. Experiment and see where you get! The lines must pick up on cue very quickly, and the worry of what is to happen is shared with the audience as each seed looks at them and then back up to the imaginary hand which is about to dip into the bag and scatter them. Acorn must make his/her first line full of the inevitability of what is about to happen, a kind of warning, that is echoed by the others. Chrysanth finishes it off with a terrified 'Fingers'!

(7) The wriggling and struggling must be confined to a small space, as if still confined in the bag, finally culminating in each one being forcibly dragged up and 'thrown' out of the bag. The order of ejection is as written, and there must appear to be an outside force and energy moving the 'seeds'. This is a very physical piece, and must be performed with energy and focus (see *'In the Bag' Workshop, Catch That Cue game*). All need to land in different, awkward positions, otherwise the audience won't believe the next section when they are supposed to be injured.

(8) Azalea takes the story line here. A 'confidential' feel works well, addressed directly to the audience.

(9) These lines are best delivered like a petulant child, and should definitely be accompanied by grimaces and extreme facial expressions.

Azalea	(*Rubbing knee exaggeratedly*) I've grazed my knee!
Chrysanth	(*Accusingly*) I've hurt my bottom!
Acorn	(*Horrified*) I've pierced my pod!
	(*All move into new grouping CS. Orchid and Azalea sitting, Chrysanth and Acorn standing behind them.*) **(11)**
Acorn	(*Menacingly. Becomes bird, wing movement in slow motion*) Oh-oh! **(11)**
Chrysanth	(*Murderously. Becomes bird wing movement in slow motion*) Oh-oh! **(11)**
Orchid	(*Quietly petrified*) Oh-oh! **(12)**
Azalea	(*Terrified*) Oh-oh!
Chrysanth and Acorn	(*Aggressively*) BIRDS! **(13)**
	(*As Birds, cover mouths of Orchid and Azalea to stifle the screams*) **(13)**
Orchid and Azalea	Aaaaaaaaargh! (*Squeals and screams, as if being picked up by birds. Freeze [tableau]*). **(14)**
Chrysanth	(*With melodramatic evil smile still as bird*) The seeds which fell on the path were eaten by birds.
All	(*Quickly back into 'Bag' positions*) **(15)**
Orchid	Once upon a time, there was a bag of seeds! **(16)**
All	(*High pitched chatter*) **(17)**
Chrysanth	What are we going to do today? **(18)**
Orchid	(*Slowly and ominously*) Out of the Bag! **(19)**
Acorn	Out of the Bag! (*looks up in horror*) Oh-oh! **(20)**
Chrysanth	Oh-oh!
Orchid	Oh-oh!

(10)   As the seeds move into the new grouping, it is best if Chrysanth and Acorn become 'birds' as they move. The tableau should focus on the vulnerability of the other two and the threatening and powerful nature of the birds. So make sure that wing movements are not feeble flaps, but powerful dramatic wing beats (slow motion could help to get this feel if the characters are having difficulty). It is a good idea when casting this to remember that Chrysanth and Acorn are helped if they are bigger than the other two characters.

(11)   Voice change required here. Definite melodramatic menace!

(12)   In contrast, the voices of Azalea and Orchid must be small and terrified as they cling to each other, waiting for the 'death blow'!

(13)   Dramatic overstatement, with much 'evil villain' melodrama, directed to the audience as they stop the screams of the others. If you are doing this sketch with young people, do warn them that it's not 'for real' and get them to work out exactly how they are going to do this move without actually suffocating their fellow actors!

(14)   Screams to be loud, and quickly stifled, with jerky movements until they are 'lifted up' by the birds. This is best achieved by them standing on tiptoe, waving their arms about and being dragged upstage into the 'bag' position.

(15)   Immediately on arrival in 'bag' area, back into original character positions, freeze momentarily, except Chrysanth, who keeps the 'Bird' character for the next line. Then a quick change, and back into 'seed position'. These moves cannot be worked out instantly, and will take much rehearsal of the 'repeat it again and again' variety to get it right.

(16)   Story telling again. All others frozen, just turn head to address audience.

(17)   (See 4)

(18)   Spoken in Children's Presenter tone.

(19)   (See 5)

(20)   (See 6)

Azalea	Oh-oh!
Chrysanth	*(Horrified, looks up as if at giant hand)* FINGERS! *(Hold on to each other, rise and fall out of bag)* **(21)**
Orchid	Some of the seed fell on to rocky ground, where there was little soil.
Azalea	I think I've fractured my skull. **(22)**
Chrysanth	*(Wriggling contentedly into position)* Find a comfortable bed!
Orchid	Oooh? I'm taking root!
Acorn	The sun slowly rose.
All	*(Move heads in unison from L to R, looking up as they blow a raspberry* **(23)**. *Then simulate great heat, fanning, puffing and blowing, etc.)* **(24)**
Chrysanth	I'm thirsty. **(25)**
Azalea	Sunstroke! **(25)**
Orchid	I've Burnt me Bud! **(25)**
Acorn	*(Sways)* I don't think I'm going to make it! *(Falls forward. All react with sad faces.)*
Acorn	*(Directly to audience)* And the heat withered the plants. **(26)**
All	*(Withering death throes)* **(27)**
Acorn	*(In a matter-of-fact tone)* And they died. *(All collapse)* **(28)** *(Quickly back into 'Bag' positions)* **(29)**
Azalea	Once upon a time, there was a bag of seeds!
All	*(High-pitched chatter)* **(30)**
Chrysanth	What are we going to do today?
Orchid	*(Slowly and fearfully)* Out of the Bag?
Acorn	Out of the Bag! *(Looks up)* Oh-oh! **(31)**
Chrysanth	Oh-oh!

(21) The fall out of the bag must be different each time, otherwise it will become boring. It is worth spending some time experimenting with different ways of doing this. Slow motion for one perhaps, if you are stuck. Imagination and physical exertion definitely *very* important here. When they fall, a 'freeze' or TABLEAU momentarily helps to focus on the story teller. You might try this every time!

(22) The 'skull' line often works well if accompanied by a rather hurt and puzzled look. Meanwhile the others are wriggling comfortably into position with pleased, surprised expressions.

(23) Move as the line is spoken.

(24) Think of different ways for each seed to show that he/she is hot. Don't allow the same reactions from all, or it won't be visually interesting.

(25) With melodramatic energy. Acorn sways with a glazed expression and falls forward. Another thing which needs rehearsal, as it needs to be slow! All watch as he falls and make the reaction BIG!

(26) Raise head with beaming grin and address the audience direct. 'Die' immediately after the line.

(27) Make a meal of this one, right over the top, but keep it short!

(28) Raise head with beaming grin and address the audience direct. 'Die' immediately after the line. The others time your final death twitch to coincide with acorn's second 'death'.

(29) The collapse should be held momentarily, then a quick move back to the 'bag'.

(30) See 4-6.

(31) See 4-6.

Orchid	Oh-oh!
Azalea	Oh-oh!
Chrysanth	*(Horrified, looks up as if at giant hand)* FINGERS! *(All roll and twist out of the 'Bag'. Noises of appreciation as they move into a row, Azalea SR, Acorn CSR, Orchid USR, Chrysanth SL.)* **(32)**
Orchid	*(Conversationally)* How's your roots? **(33)**
Azalea	*(Confidently)* I feel quite solid!
Orchid	*(Surprised)* OW! . . . Sprouting. *(Shoots left hand into air)*
Azalea	Oooh. *(Leg shoots up suddenly. Orchid and Azalea continue to 'sprout'.)* **(34)**
Acorn	Some seeds fell on soil where WEEEEEDS grow. **(35)** *(Acorn and Chrysanth crouch down and grow with evil laughs, Orchid and Azalea continue to grow, cheerful, smug and unaware of the danger.)*
Chrysanth	*(Gleefully choking them as they speak)* And choked them! **(36)**
	(Acorn and Chrysanth slap hands in victory. Azalea dies. Orchid shrivels) **(37)**
Orchid	*(Weakly)* Aaaaargh! *(Dies)*
	(All quickly back into 'Bag' positions) **(38)**
Chrysanth	Once upon a time, there was a bag of seeds!
All	*(High-pitched chatter)*
Chrysanth	What are we going to do today?
Orchid	*(Slowly and ominously)* Out of the Bag. **(39)**
Acorn	Out of the Bag! *(Looks up)* Oh-oh!
Chrysanth	Oh-oh!
Orchid	Oh-oh!

58

(32)   Use low levels for this one, twisted shapes too.

(33)   Very conversational tone important here, and a development of gradual confidence, especially in Orchid and Azalea.

(34)   These movements must be full of energy, imaginative, and the facial expression should show pleasant shock and surprise.

(35)   'Weeds', with a fully extended 'eeeee' sound, and as the word is said, a change of character again for Acorn and Chrysanth, which will be mainly shown by body shape. As boisterous, mischievous, slightly evil children. Facial expression, body shape, voice, all contribute to the overall sense of being attacked by a wicked but quite attractive imp.

(36)   The smug expressions of Azalea and Orchid lend themselves to an audience reaction in sympathy with the weeds, and produces a sort of 'anti-hero' humour.

(37)   As Azalea dies instantly, Orchid struggles a little and then slowly and gracefully shrivels, like an Edwardian heroine!

(38)   Very quick and accurate and don't forget the momentary freeze.

(39)   See first section.

Azalea	Oh-oh!
Chrysanth	*(Horrified, looks up as if at giant hand)* FINGERS!
	(All slowly move as if being pulled out of bag) **(40)**
Azelea	*(Smugly)* I'm prepared. **(41)**
Orchid	*(Cheerfully)* Send you a postcard! **(42)**
Chrysanth	*(Matter of fact)* Packed lunch! **(42)**
Acorn	*(Contentedly)* A warm flask of wine! **(42)**
	(All fall) **(43)**
Chrysanth	Some seeds fell on GOOD soil!
All	*(Wriggle into row, sounds of pleasure, Azelea SR, Acorn CSR, Orchid CSL, Chrysanth SL.)*
Orchid	Ooooooh! I'm sinking REALLY deep!
Acorn	*(Ecstatically)* Oh My!
Chrysanth	*(Shivers with delight)*
Orchid	*(Proud)* I can see it now! I'm going to be . . . an Orchid!
Azelea	*(Excited)* An Azelea!
Chrysanth	*(Self-satisfied)* A Chrysanthemum!
Acorn	*(Wildly ecstatic)* A Tree! **(44)**
All	*(All freeze in final tableau)* And we all increased **(45)**
Orchid	Thirtyfold!
Azelea	Fiftyfold!
Chrysanth	Eightyfold!
Acorn	One HUNDREDfold!
	(Frozen tableau) **(46)**

(40)   The resistance to being pulled out of the bag should appear the same each time the sequence arises, and by this time the seeds are becoming quite used to their mishaps, and indeed should convey a fairly smug feeling.

(41)   Azalea, to audience, *very* smug.

(42)   Excitedly childlike, as if going on a holiday to which s/he has looked forward for a long time. Each character should have a contrasting reaction. Most importantly, they all fall in slow motion while they are speaking and land on good soil at exactly the same time. This unity of action provides a basis for much of the humour. Freeze the action momentarily during the line, 'Some seeds fell on good soil'.

(43)   As they wriggle and sink with ecstatic noises, the dialogue continues. Once they realise their potential, the pace should be speeded up, *not* of the actual lines, but the jumping in.

(44)   It is important that Tree (Acorn) makes an expansive movement with the whole of the body which is made simultaneously with the length of the word 'Treeeee'. Finish finally with a wild and fixed gleeful expression.

(45)   As the group go into the freeze, it is effective if they too make an expansive movement just prior to the freeze, finishing with fixed gleeful expressions. As they speak their lines it works well if they quickly come out of freeze and address the audience and then swiftly return to the tableau position and expression. When 'Tree' says his/her line, it should be with wild abandon, all the others momentarily, and *exactly* together, turn heads to glare at him, and then back to tableau, as Tree, smilingly shamefaced, returns to his place, and suddenly, in rebellion, wildly resumes his freeze as before.

(46)   Hold the tableau for 3-5 seconds before exiting.

Glossary

Blocking   Roughly planning out the moves within the stage area, and pencilling them in the script. Be flexible, they may have to be changed.

CS   *(Centre Stage)* A position right in the centre of the acting area.

CSL   *(Centre Stage Left)* A position a little to the left of the centre of the acting area.

CSR   *(Centre Stage Right)* A position a little to the right of the centre of the acting area.

Cue   A word or visual signal of some kind which indicates either a reaction or another move or response from an actor or technician.

DSC   *(Down Stage Centre)* A position in the middle at the front of the acting area nearest to the audience.

DSCL   *(Down Stage Centre Left)* A position at the front of the acting area left of centre.

DSCR   *(Down Stage Centre Right)* A position at the front of the acting area right of centre.

DSL   *(Down Stage Left)* A position at the extreme left of the acting area, at the front, nearest the audience.

DSR   *(Down Stage Right)* A position at the extreme right of the acting area, at the front, nearest the audience.

Focus   *1* The words or actions upon which you wish the audience to concentrate.

    2 The concentrated attitude of the actor bent upon his task, without being distracted.

    3 The highest physical point of energy of an action.

Freeze   Suspended animation, total stillness, usually focused on a point of energy.

Freeze Frame   Suspended animation of a group of actors, rather like the 'stills' in a film sequence.

Levels   A series of positions in the acting area, which places the actors in a visually interesting position in relation one to another and also creates focus, and reveals status in their relationships as characters.

Masking   One actor standing in front of another and preventing the audience from seeing or focusing where they should.

Mime   Action without words.

Neutral   This involves standing still and relaxed, with feet slightly apart, to give good balance. When in neutral there should be a stillness, and a sense of just being there without making any statement to distract from the action. Complete stillness and relaxation is the order of the day. It's a bit like the breathing and relaxation in an upright position!

Quick Pics   A small frozen group tableau representing a scene, situation or idea.

SL   *(Stage Left)* A position to the extreme left of the centre of the acting area.

SR   *(Stage Right)* A position to the extreme right of the centre of the acting area.

Stage Directions

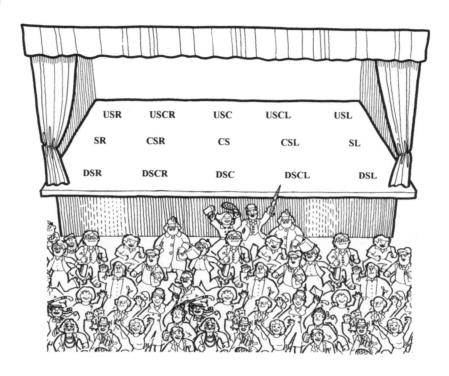

Tableau   A still group picture.

USC   *(Up Stage Centre)* A position at the centre back of the acting area.

USCL   *(Up Stage Centre Left)* A position at the back of the acting area and slightly to the left.

USCR   *(Up Stage Centre Right)* A position at the back of the acting area and slightly to the right when facing the audience.

USL   *(Up Stage Left)* A position at the back of the acting area to the extreme left of centre, when facing the audience.

USR   *(Up Stage Right)* A position at the back of the acting area to the extreme right of centre, when facing the audience.

WIP   *(Walking Into Pictures)* An exercise where the whole group creates a picture, as if in a frame on a given theme, concentrating on relationships between the actors within their situation. It must be an interesting visual communication. It must accurately communicate the theme, and show thoughtfulness by the actors in terms of their positioning and levels and their sensitivity to the action and mime of others.

Father Abraham